# Buried in The Darkness

*The Darkbound Saga*
*Book 1 of 5*

By Grayson Sharp

# Buried in the Darkness
*Book One of the Darkbound Saga*

© 2025 Grayson Sharp
Published by Darkbound Publishing

ISBN (Paperback): 979-8-9999396-0-9
ISBN (Hardcover): 979-8-9999396-1-6

Cover design by Grayson Sharp
Printed in the United States of America

First Edition

# Table of Contents

# Trigger Warnings

Violence

Possible torture

Hints at suicide

Kidnapping

Possible sexual assault

Psychological trauma

Mental Disassociation

Strong language

# Inspiration Playlist

Beg (On Your Knees) - Ash to Eden
Under My Skin - Ash to Eden
Underneath - Phix & Ryan Oakes
Gojo (The Honored One) - 7emralds
Alone With You - Bryce Savage
Long Hair and Some Tattoos - Bryce Savage
Curiosity - Bryce Savage
Cowbell Warrior! - SXMPRA
Popular Monster - Falling in Reverse
Outrunning - Ryan Jesse
Trainwreck - Ryan Jesse
Shallow - Magnolia Park
Addict - Don Louis

# Prologue

I'm the one you meet first. Tall, about 6'4" with dark black shaggy hair, just long enough to shadow my eyes. Thank God I let my hair grow. Sky blue starburst eyes are hard to hide.

Do you have any idea the amount of people that will walk up and stare at someone like me? I guess it would be the darker tawny brown skin in contrast to my eye color. But still, didn't their parents ever teach them not to stare.

Anyways, like I was saying, I'm sort of the front man. I keep everything running smooth. I have the smile, the quick wit, the easy conversation — that's all me. You'd think you're talking to him, but you're not. He's somewhere in the background, quiet, watching, letting me take the wheel.

I speak fast, I move first, I decide without hesitation. Where he pauses, I cut through. Where he worries, I act. People like to think that makes me reckless. They're wrong. I'm calculated. Every move has weight, even the ones that look careless.

There are... others here.

We don't all see the world the same way, and not all of us are fit for daylight. I am. I wear the grin, shake the hands, make the deals. I keep the peace until peace doesn't work anymore.

Sometimes, when the air changes — when a certain switch flips — I feel him watching me. Not him... the other one. The one with no name. The one who waits in silence until he's called. You wouldn't know him if you passed him in the street. You'd just feel the weight in your chest. That... predator's stillness.

I've let him out before. Briefly.

Once you've seen him move, you don't forget it. Neither do the people who've been on the other end of his attention.

But most days, it's just me at the wheel.

I'm the driver, the face, the negotiator. The one who keeps us running smoothly.

And as long as I'm here, as long as things go the way I plan, you'll never have to meet the others.

# The Stranger

*Jace pov*

New York in early winter doesn't whisper. It bites. The kind of cold that cuts through gloves, slides down your collar, and makes every breath feel like chewing glass. I keep my head down and my pace steady, letting the city's chaos move around me instead of through me.

Most people here walk with a destination in mind. Tonight, I don't have one. I'm moving just to move — a habit that keeps the thoughts from getting too loud.

That's when I see her. Same skin complexion as mine, high cheek bones. Long auburn, no red, wait...it's like a mix between both. She couldn't be taller than 5'4" maybe. But what steals my attention the most is her eyes. How could someone capture the sun in their eyes? So bright, so warm.

She's not dressed for the weather. No one sane would be. Thin coat, no hat, standing still while the whole world rushes around her. People glance, then look away. New Yorkers are experts at ignoring what doesn't concern them.

But something about her won't let me pass.

Not because she's beautiful — though she is — but because she's still. Perfectly still. Like the wind doesn't touch her.

The others inside me notice before I do.

Michael shifts in his seat, leaning forward. Lucian doesn't move, but I feel that slow, steady awareness turn in her direction.

I stop a few paces away, close enough that I can study her without raising alarms. She doesn't look up right away, but when she does, her eyes lock on mine like she was expecting me. No flicker of surprise. No polite smile. Just...stillness.

"Lost?" I ask. My voice is even, casual — the kind of tone you use with strangers who might not want to be approached.

She shakes her head. "Waiting."

"For someone?"

Her lips curve, but it's not quite a smile. "Maybe."

Michael perks up, interested now. *She's quick. No stutter, no hesitation.* I feel him leaning forward, testing her in his own way without speaking aloud.

Lucian doesn't comment. He doesn't need to. His attention feels heavier than mine — like a weight pressing from the inside. She doesn't flinch under it, though.

"You'll freeze out here," I say. "This city eats people like that alive."

"I'm not that easy to chew," she replies.

There it is — the hook. The air between us shifts, just slightly. I don't know her, but I know the kind of people who say things like that and mean them. They're rare.

And somewhere, deep inside, Lucian moves one step closer to the glass.

The wind cuts harder, pushing people along the sidewalk like cattle, but she stands rooted. I glance over her shoulder and spot the neon glow of a café sign half a block away.

"Come on," I say, tilting my head toward it. "At least get warm while you... wait."

She studies me like she's weighing the risk. Then, without a word, she falls into step beside me.

The café is almost empty, the kind of place that smells like burnt espresso and old wood. A couple in the corner talks in low voices. A tired-looking barista glances up and doesn't bother with a greeting. We slid into a booth near the window, the glass fogging from the sudden heat.

I take off my gloves, watching her across the table. "So... who's worth freezing for?"

Her eyes narrow slightly. "Maybe no one."

Michael chuckles inside my head. *She's playing. Push back, but don't spook her.*

I lean back. "Maybe? That's a long time to stand still just to find out."

"Not everyone you wait for is someone you want to see," she says. Her voice is calm, but there's something sharp under it — something deliberate.

The waitress drops off two mugs without asking for our order. The coffee's black, bitter, perfect for stalling.

I wrap my hands around the cup. "So do I get to call you 'mystery woman,' or is there a name that comes with all this frostbite?"

Her gaze holds mine. "Names have weight. You don't just give them to anyone."

Michael leans in now, smirking. *Alright, my turn.*

*No, let me handle this.* I say to Michael. Damn he's pushy sometimes.

I let a half-smile tug at my mouth. "Fine. I'll earn it. Give me one thing about you, and I'll give you one about me."

Her head tilts slightly. "And if I lie?"

"Then I'll know."

A beat passes, and then — "Madison."

It lands like she's testing the sound in my ears.

I nod, letting it roll around in my head. "Madison what?"

She looks past me toward the window, as if considering whether I've earned it. Then, with a shrug so casual it's almost dismissive: "Hawks."

I take a slow sip of coffee, letting her name linger in my head. Madison Hawks. It fits her — uncommon, deliberate, a little dangerous.

"So," I say, setting the cup down, "why the sidewalk meditation in subzero wind?"

She traces her fingertip along the rim of her mug, eyes dropping to the coffee like she's deciding how much to tell. "I was waiting for someone I wasn't sure would come."

"An old friend?"

"Not exactly."

"Enemy?"

Her lips twitch. "Closer."

Michael perks up at that. *Closer to the enemy? That's interesting.*

Part of me wants to press. But the way she's holding herself — relaxed shoulders, slow blink — it's bait, and she knows it.

"Did they show?" I ask.

Her gaze lifts, locks with mine. "They're sitting across from me right now."

For half a second, everything inside me stills. Michael goes silent. I try to process the words. And way down in the dark, something colder stirs — a faint shift, like chains settling.

I blink, keeping my voice even. "You were waiting for me?"

"I didn't know your face," she says. "But I'd know the way you walk anywhere."

That's when I feel it — not Lucian, not Michael, but a trace of something heavier pressing against the glass from the inside. HIM isn't awake... but he's listening.

I force my voice steady. "You've been watching me?"

"Not you," she says, tapping the table once with her fingertip. "All of you."

Michael straightens, intrigued now. "All of who?" I ask.

She tilts her head, eyes glinting like she knows exactly what she's doing. "You'll tell me when you're ready."

The faint draft from deep inside fades, like whatever was listening has stepped back into the dark. But the echo of it stays in my bones.

I take another sip of coffee, slower this time. "You're a strange woman, Madison Hawks."

She smiles again, small and sure. "And you're not one man."

The coffee's gone cold by the time we stand. The air outside hits like a slap, sharp and dry, but it's nothing compared to the static still buzzing between us.

We fall into step without talking. New York hums around us — the hiss of buses, the thud of boots on frozen pavement, the distant wail of a siren. I keep my eyes forward, but I can feel her glance at me every few strides.

"You're quiet now," she says.

"Processing."

"Me?"

"You," I say, "and the fact you're apparently keeping a running tab on all my... sides."

Michael grins in my head. *Ease in. Don't make her defensive. But don't let her skate either.*

"You make it sound like I'm doing something wrong," she says.

"Depends on how you got the information."

She tucks her hands in her coat pockets. "It wasn't hard. One of you introduced himself to me, remember?"

I stopped walking. "When?"

She stops too, and there's that curve to her lips again — not a smile, not a smirk. "Oh, you don't remember."

The hair on the back of my neck prickles. Michael goes still.

"I've had a lot of nights," I say carefully.

"This one," she says, "was different. Louder. Messier. One of you was... unraveling. I thought for a second I'd meet the one you never let out. But instead—" she shrugs "—I met the other one."

The way she says *the other one* lands heavy. Not Lucian's

name, but enough to make HIM stir faintly in the background, like a shadow brushing my shoulder.

We start walking again, slower now. "You sure you're not confusing me with someone else?"

Her breath leaves her in a fogged laugh. "I'm sure. That night, you were..." She glances sideways at me, studying my posture, the set of my jaw. "Different. More deliberate. Every move you made was measured. The way you spoke—" she trails off, smirking "—it wasn't you. Not this version of you, anyway."

Michael's voice is tight in my head. *She's describing Lucian.*

"Maybe I just had too much to drink," I say.

"You did," she says. "Both of you did."

Both. The word hits like a pebble in my gut.

She keeps talking. "I remember thinking the night was about to spiral into something you couldn't walk away from. You... he—" she corrects herself, "—stepped in before it went that far."

Her tone shifts on that last part. Not admiration, exactly. More like... interest.

Michael cuts in. *She knows man. She saw him. And she's not afraid.*

I shove my hands in my pockets to keep them still. "What happened after?"

Her eyes flicker, just for a second. "Maybe I'll tell you when I'm sure you want the answer."

The light changes, and she steps into the crosswalk before I can reply. I follow, the cold biting harder now.

When we reach the opposite curb, she stops under a streetlamp, the yellow light haloing her hair. "You're trying to figure out if I'm dangerous," she says.

"I'm trying to figure out what you are."

She smiles — slow, deliberate. "Good. Keep trying."

She turns then, disappearing into the crowd like she belongs to it. I stand there long enough for the cold to creep down my collar before Michael finally speaks again.

*We need to find out what she knows. And fast.*

I nod once, though no one's looking. *Yeah,* I murmur. *Before I find out the hard way.*

# Reflections

The apartment is dark except for the light over the bathroom sink. I'm still wearing my coat, breath steaming faintly in the cold air seeping through the old window.

The mirror's streaked from the last time I wiped it down, but my reflection's clear enough.

*She knows something,* I say to the mirror. Though I know they're listening, they always are.

Michael leans forward from the other side — not physically, but I see him in the set of my jaw, the slight curl of my lip. *She knows more than she's saying.*

*Lucian,* I murmur. *She's seen him.*

*And she didn't flinch,* Michael says. *That's what bothers me.*

I grip the edge of the sink, leaning closer. *That night... I can't remember it. Not all of it.*

*Because you weren't there for all of it. Not really anyways.*

The words land heavy in the space between us.

*Then who was?*

Michael's reflection smirks faintly. *You already know. We were slipping. HIM was close. Lucian stepped in.*

I shake my head. *Why?*

*To keep HIM down where he belongs. You remember the last time he got out... we all suffered. And others.* Michael says.

The faucet drips once, the sound loud in the silence.

*She said we were both drinking.* I mutter. *Both of us. That means you were there before he was. I don't even remember going to the bar? Was I drinking before you took over?*

*Yeah. Dealing with the anniversary of the accident still gets to you, well not just you, all of us.* Michael says. A hint of sorrow edged in his voice.

*And yes, I felt him coming up through the cracks.* His tone hardens. *I didn't have the control to stop it. He did.*

I straighten slowly. *So she's seen the mask.* I say more as a statement.

*Maybe more than that?*

I stare at my own eyes in the glass. *Then we find out what she knows. Everything.*

Michael's grin widens. *Now you're talking.*

I leave the bathroom light on as I walk into the living room. The apartment feels too quiet, like the walls are listening. I drop onto the couch, pull my phone from my pocket, and stare at her number.

Michael is already pacing inside my head. *Don't just ask her outright. Make her come to you.*

I hover my thumb over the screen. *What do I even say?*

*Something that sounds casual but makes her lean forward when she reads it.*

*And if she ignores it?*

*Then she's not who we think she is.*

The last time I played this game, I overplayed my hand. The memory ends badly — for me, for the other guy, for anyone in the blast radius. HIM had been close then too.

I take a breath and type four words: "We need to talk."

Michael snorts. *That's a demand, not bait.*

*Good.*

*Add a place. Somewhere open enough for you to feel safe...but not too open.*

I delete the text, retype: "Midnight. Penn Station. South

Concourse." Then hit send before I can think about it.

The read receipt comes almost instantly. No reply.

*She's going to show,* I say.

*Yeah? And how do you know?*

*Because people who know something dangerous don't ignore invitations to talk about it.*

I lean back, eyes on the dark ceiling. There's a faint pulse at the base of my skull — not pain, just... pressure.

*He's listening again,* Michael mutters.

I don't answer. Because I already know.

The hours crawl. I try the TV. Can't focus. Try music. Too loud. The clock on the wall sounds like it's ticking straight into my skull.

Michael is pacing again, more restless than before.

*She's going to make us wait until the last possible second. Bet on it.*

I glance at my phone — no reply. Just that read receipt staring back at me like an unblinking eye.

*Maybe she's not coming.*

*Oh, she's coming,* Michael says. *People like her can't resist a dangling thread.*

The pressure in the back of my skull sharpens. Not pain. Not exactly. It's the same feeling as before, that heavy awareness pressing against the inside.

And then I hear him — not HIM, not yet — but the low, even voice of Lucian, threading through the static in my head.

*I've got him... for now.*

The words are so clear it feels like they're whispered right behind my ear. I swallow hard.

*Do you feel that?* I ask Michael.

*Yeah,* he mutters. *Means he's close enough to taste the air.*

I pace the apartment, checking the time again. 11:42 p.m. Too early to leave, too late to distract myself. My palms are damp, and I hate that they are.

Lucian cuts in again, steady, controlled. *Focus on the meeting. Nothing else. I'll keep him calm.*

*Not exactly reassuring,* I mutter.

*Wasn't meant to be,* he replies. Then he's gone again, fading back into that silent space he lives in until I call him.

By the time I step out into the night, the cold feels sharper. The streets are thinner now, fewer people, more shadows.

Michael is quiet for the first few blocks. Then, *what if she's here to pull HIM out?*

*She wouldn't survive it,* I say.

*Maybe she's not planning to.*

That thought sticks with me all the way to Penn Station.

The South Concourse is a wash of harsh fluorescent lights and echoing footsteps. I pick a spot near one of the pillars where I can see both entrances.

11:59. My pulse is a little too fast.

Michael leans forward in my head. *Eyes up. She's here.*

And then I see her — Madison, weaving through the sparse crowd, coat open just enough to show she's not freezing, gaze locked straight on me.

She moves through the crowd like the rest of the world isn't even there — eyes locked, pace steady, never breaking stride. I feel Michael straighten inside, all sharp edges now.

When she stops in front of me, there's no hello. No small

talk.

"You don't remember what you did, do you?"

The words land like a body blow.

Not what happened. Not that night. What I did.

I keep my face still, but inside, Michael leans forward fast. *Don't bite yet. Let her talk.*

"Depends on the night," I say evenly.

She tilts her head, reading me like a page. "You were wearing the 'mask'. Your voice wasn't yours. And you looked at me like you were deciding whether to ruin me... or save me."

That faint pulse at the base of my skull slams harder. HIM is stirring again. And then, sliding in like a calm hand on my shoulder, Lucian's voice: *Breathe. I've got him.*

I shift my stance, forcing air into my lungs. "You seem pretty sure that was me."

Her mouth curves, just a little. "Oh, it wasn't you. Not this you."

Michael's tone is low now, almost wary. *She's baiting us. She wants a reaction.*

Madison steps closer, so close I can smell the faint trace of smoke and winter air in her hair. "The part I can't decide," she says softly, "is whether he came out because you wanted him to... or because you were afraid of what was underneath him."

The temperature in my head drops a degree. Lucian's presence stays firm, but I feel the chains shift in the dark.

*She's getting too close,* Michael warns.

I step back just enough to break the moment. "You want to tell me what happened that night, or keep dancing around it?"

She smiles — slow, deliberate. "Oh, I'll tell you. But not all at once. You'd ruin the ending."

And with that, she brushes past me, heading for the exit like she owns the timing.

I turn to follow her, the sound of her boots sharp against the tile. She doesn't look back until she's almost at the exit.

"You know," she says over her shoulder, "you didn't hesitate when you put your hands on me. Not even when I was bleeding."

I freeze.

Bleeding.

The word snaps something inside like a frayed cable. The pulse at the base of my skull turns into a pounding, steady and deep. HIM isn't just stirring now — he's leaning against the glass.

Michael's voice is suddenly tight. *Wait—what the hell is she talking about?*

The pounding grows heavier, the air in my head thickening with it. HIM isn't angry. He's alert. Watching. Protective.

Madison takes a step closer again, her voice lower this time. "You didn't even ask who hurt me. You just... handled it."

That's when Michael stops talking entirely — like a man who knows the next step is past his pay grade.

Lucian's voice cuts in, cold and precise. *I'll take it from here.*

The pounding eases, but only just. HIM is still there, close enough that I can feel the weight of him.

Madison sees something shift in my eyes and smiles faintly. "There it is," she murmurs.

Something changes in the air between us — like a door closing behind me. My breathing slows, my shoulders loosen, and every movement becomes deliberate. I feel the calm settle in, the kind that only comes when Lucian is steering.

(Lucian pov)

Madison tilts her head, watching me like she's confirming a suspicion. "There you are," she says softly.

I don't answer right away. I take a step toward her, slow enough to feel the click of my boots on the tile. My voice, when it comes, is lower, steadier. "You've been playing with HIM. That's dangerous."

Her eyes don't waver. "I wasn't playing."

"You were testing boundaries," I say, "to see which one would come out. You got close to the wrong answer."

She smirks, but there's a flicker in her eyes — not fear, not exactly, but recognition. "And yet here you are, not him."

The pounding in my head has dulled, but it hasn't gone away. HIM is still there, pacing. Waiting.

I take another step, closing the space between us until I can feel her breath in the cold air. "If he had come out," I say evenly, "we wouldn't be having this conversation. You'd be somewhere safe... or they'd still be cleaning up the mess."

Her smile fades just slightly. "So, you're the leash."

"I'm the line," I correct. "And you're standing on it."

For the first time, she glances away, just briefly, before turning toward the station doors. "Midnight's over," she says. "We'll talk again."

She leaves without looking back.

I stay there a moment longer, feeling HIM's presence slowly drift backward into the dark. Not gone — never gone — but contained.

For now. I follow suit, deciding to let someone else take the wheel. My presence isn't really needed for everyday use wink* wink*.

Michaels is more than eager to take the lead.

(Michael)

By the time we're outside, the cold is nothing compared to the static still rattling around in my head. Jace is there, but he's heavy — worn out, the way you get after barely holding the line.

I got it from here, I tell him.

*Fine* he mutters inside, voice flat. *Just... don't push her too hard.*

She's already halfway down the block when I start after her, keeping my pace casual. The city's quieter now, the kind of quiet that makes every footstep sound louder than it should.

"You've got a way of showing up just to light matches," I called out.

She glances over her shoulder, slows, but doesn't stop. "I thought you liked fire."

"Depends on who's holding the match."

We fall into stride, me a step behind. Jace's watching from inside, still catching his breath.

*She knew about HIM,* he said quietly in my head. *She was trying to get him out.*

*Yeah,* I reply, keeping my tone neutral outwardly. *And she almost did.*

Madison finally stops, turns to face me. "You're not the same one I was talking to a few minutes ago."

I give her a half-smile. "You notice too much for your own good."

"Maybe. Or maybe you want me to."

"Or maybe," I say, stepping a little closer, "you're forgetting there's a line between curiosity and suicide."

She studies me for a beat, then shakes her head like she's disappointed. "I'm not afraid of him."

Jace stirs at that, a faint ripple of tension in the back of my mind.

"You should be," I say.

Her smirk is back, faint but deliberate. "Then maybe I'm exactly where I'm supposed to be."

Before I can push her further, she turns and melts into the crowd again, leaving me with the same questions we walked in with — and a feeling I don't like.

She's not running from HIM.

She's circling him.

I don't follow her this time. No point. She's already decided how far tonight goes.

The walk back to the apartment is slow, deliberate. Every step gives me room to think — and room for Jace to talk from the back seat.

*She's too confident,* he says. *Not just in knowing... in surviving it.*

*Yeah,* I reply. *And that means she's either stupid or she's holding something that makes her feel untouchable.*

We hit the corner near my building. The streetlight's buzzing overhead, casting a sick yellow glow on the sidewalk. I glance up out of habit, scanning the rooftops. No reason. Just... habit.

*Lucian said she was testing boundaries,* Jace adds.

*He wasn't wrong. She's circling HIM. But here's the thing, Jace — she's doing it without fear. And that's either bravado or experience.*

*Experience.* he says, almost certain.

The apartment feels colder than outside when I step in. I shrug out of my coat, drop into the chair by the window, and look at the reflection in the glass.

*Next move?* Jace asks.

*We don't chase her directly, I say. She's expecting that. We find the night.*

*You mean—*

*We go back. Bars. Alleys. People who might've seen us. Something will crack.*

*That's risky. If HIM was that close, someone might've noticed.*

*Then we're careful who we ask. We talk to the ones who don't care about the truth — they care about the story.*

I lean forward, resting my elbows on my knees. *And when she finally tells us?*

Jace exhales slowly. *We make sure she's telling it to the right version of us.*

For the first time tonight, a smile tugs at my mouth. *Exactly.*

But even as I say it, I feel that faint, slow pacing in the dark corner of my mind. HIM hasn't gone back to sleep yet.

# Bars

The first bar is a hole in the wall wedged between a laundromat and a pawn shop, the kind of place that smells like stale beer no matter what time of day you walk in.

The neon sign in the window says OPEN, but it feels like the kind of open that's more of a dare than an invitation.

I push through the door. Same cracked leather booths. Same uneven floor. Same guy behind the bar.

Jackson.

Jack to anyone who's been here more than once.

He's wiping down the counter with a rag that's seen better decades, his bulk leaning forward just enough to make him look like he owns the place. He glances up, squints, then grins slowly.

"Well, well. Look who finally crawled back out of the woodwork."

"Been a while," I say, sliding onto a stool.

Jack tosses the rag over his shoulder. "Yeah. Last time you were in here, you didn't leave alone."

Jace stirs in the back of my head. *He remembers something.*

"Who was I with?" I ask.

Jack's grin widens, like he's about to enjoy this. "Some woman. Dark coat, boots. Sharp eyes. Didn't say much, but she didn't have to."

Madison.

Jack leans in. "Thing is... you weren't yourself that night. Not the guy I'm talking to now. Hell, not even the other one I've seen in here once or twice."

I still. *Of course he knows about us.*

Jack points a thick finger at me. "No. This was someone else. Quieter. But... heavier. Made the air feel different. People got out of your way without knowing why."

Lucian.

"What happened?" I ask.

Jack shrugs. "Couple guys came in, got rowdy. You didn't yell, didn't swing. Just looked at 'em. Like you were deciding something. Next thing I know, they're gone, she's bleeding, and you're walking her out without a word."

Jace's voice is tight. *Bleeding again.*

Jack grabs a bottle from the shelf, pours me a glass without asking. "Never saw you like that before. Hope I don't again."

Jack sets the bottle down, his eyes narrowing just slightly. "You know... you keep walking the way you've been walking, one day it's not gonna be you I see come through that door."

The way he says it isn't a joke. It's flat, certain.

Jace's presence in my head stiffens instantly. *What does he mean by that?*

Before I can answer him, Jack adds, "Next time, it won't be the quiet one either. It'll be the one you've been burying. And when he shows up... somebody's not walking back out."

The pulse in my skull jumps, hot and sharp. HIM is awake enough to listen now.

Jace's voice spikes hard in my head. *I'm taking this.*

*Wait—*

Too late. It's like getting yanked backwards out of my own body — no warning, just the world snapping into a slightly different focus as Jace plants both hands on the bar.

(Jace pov)

"You don't know what you're talking about," I say evenly.

Jack just smirks, slow and steady. "Sure I don't."

Inside, Michael crosses his arms and leans against the wall of my own head. *Really, Jace? Couldn't let me finish my drink first?*

*Not when you're about to make it worse,* I mutter under my breath.

*You're a buzzkill.*

*Deal with it.*

Jack turns away, busying himself with stacking glasses like the conversation never happened. But his last words stick — not just with Michael, not just with me... but with the thing pacing in the dark.

The cold outside hits harder after the warmth of the bar. My breath hangs in the air in short bursts as I shove my hands into my pockets and start walking.

Jack's words won't leave my head.

*It won't be you... it'll be the one you've been burying.*

HIM is still there, faint but steady, like a shadow keeping

pace beside me that no one else can see.

Michael finally speaks up, his voice dripping with mock annoyance. *Nice. Real smooth, Jace. Now he's thinking about you more than me.*

*I had to shut it down.*

*You had to overreact,* he shoots back. *You know I had that under control. I was gonna ease him into giving us more. But nooo... you had to grab the wheel and white-knuckle it like a dad on his first icy road trip.*

*Jack was trying to pull HIM into the conversation.*

*Exactly. Which is why you don't let him see he got to you. You keep him thinking he's in charge, and he tells you everything just to feel smart.*

I keep walking, the glow from the streetlights casting long, distorted shadows on the sidewalk. My shadow doesn't feel like mine right now.

*He was right about one thing,* I say quietly.

*Oh, this I gotta hear.*

*If HIM shows up... somebody's not walking back out.*

Michael's chuckle is low, dark, almost fond. *Yeah. And I'm not sure if that should scare me or make me feel better.*

We turn down my block, the apartment lights just ahead. The weight in my head hasn't gone away. HIM isn't slipping back into the dark tonight — he's staying close enough to watch.

And I hate that a part of me feels safer because of it.

The city sounds different in the morning — softer, like it's trying not to wake itself.

Steam curls from the radiator by the window, carrying that faint metallic smell I've never been able to ignore. My coffee sits untouched on the table.

HIM's weight is still in my head. Not loud, not pushing — just... there.

Watching.

I run a hand over my face, feeling the grit of a half-slept night. Michael is quiet for once, probably sulking over the way I yanked the wheel last night. But his silence isn't peaceful; it's the kind of quiet a dog makes when it's watching something on the other side of the fence.

The phone on the counter buzzes once.

unknown number.

No message — just the kind of missed call that feels intentional.

I let it go.

The mirror by the door catches me on the way to the kitchen. I stop. My reflection looks more awake than I feel. That's never a good sign.

*You're not gonna eat?* Michael finally pipes up, his voice rough from disuse.

*Not hungry.*

*You will be when he decides to burn through whatever's keeping him in the backseat.*

I take a sip of cold coffee and warm up a bagel just to shut him up. *He's not coming out.*

*That's cute. You think you're deciding that.*

The radiator hisses like it's laughing with him.

By the time I pull on my jacket, the city's already moving — cabs sliding past, boots slapping wet pavement, the distant sound of a construction drill chewing through metal. I don't have a plan, but sitting still feels worse than walking blind.

Half a block from my place, I spot her.

Madison.

Across the street, leaning against a mailbox like she's been there long enough to decide whether to cross.

She notices me the second I see her, and that faint smirk curves her mouth. Not wide enough for the crowd to notice, but enough to make the hairs at my neck stand.

"Are you following me now?" I call across.

She shrugs. "Maybe I'm just... around."

The walk sign changes. She steps into the street without looking, eyes never leaving mine.

Michael mutters low in my head. *This is either about last night... or she's here to poke the cage again.*

I step forward to meet her halfway.

She stops just close enough that I can smell the cold on her coat.

"Rough night?" she asks, like she already knows the answer.

"Didn't sleep much."

"Thinking about what Jack said?"

I don't ask how she knows. That would give her too much.

Instead, I study her face — calm, but not careless. Like she's walking a tightrope she's been on before.

"Jack talks too much," I say.

Her lips curve faintly. "Only when he thinks the person listening needs to hear it."

Michael leans in from inside. *She's not just fishing — she's measuring you.*

I let a beat of silence stretch before speaking. "You could've called instead of waiting out here."

"I could've," she says, "but then I wouldn't get to see how you look in daylight."

"And?"

Her eyes flicker, just enough for me to catch it. "You look like you're still deciding which one of you I'm talking to."

I take a slow step past her, motioning with my head for her to walk. She falls in beside me, unhurried.

"You ever think," she says after a moment, "that maybe you're not the only one with... compartments?"

That lands heavier than I want it to.

"What's your point?"

"No point." She shrugs, glancing at a passing bus. "Just... maybe you're not the only one who can decide who comes to the surface."

Michael shifts in my head, tone dry. *She's not lying.*

The street noise swells as we turn the corner — brakes squealing, a radio blaring somewhere above. I wait until we're clear of the crowd before speaking again.

"If that's true," I say, "then you should know what you're doing when you talk like that."

"Oh," she says, smiling now, "I know exactly what I'm doing."

We stop at the curb, the crosswalk light still red. She doesn't look at me, just watches the traffic pass, hands in her pockets.

Without turning, she says, "I'm free tonight."

It's not an invitation.

It's a move.

The light changes. She crosses without waiting for me.

I catch up to her halfway down the block.

"You didn't say where," I point out.

"You'll know when it's time."

The way she says it sits wrong.

Too sure. Too rehearsed.

We reach the next corner and she stops, glancing at her phone before sliding it back into her coat pocket. "See you tonight, Jace."

Not we. Not you guys. Just me.

Michael huffs. *She's playing favorites now.*

I watch her disappear into the crowd before turning back toward my place. The air feels heavier the closer I get, like something waiting at the edge of my thoughts.

By the time I step inside, I know he's there. Quiet. Listening.

Lucian's voice threads through the static.

*The night she's talking about... you weren't the one holding her up when she was bleeding.*

I stop in the middle of the room.

*Then who was?*

There's a pause, like he's sifting through his own memory.

*She didn't see HIM. Not fully. But she saw what came right before him.*

Michael stiffens instantly. *The fuck does that mean?*

Lucian ignores him.

*She saw the shift. She heard the voice. And she stayed.*

I feel that drop in my gut — the kind you get when you realize the danger wasn't enough to make someone run.

*She stayed?* I repeat.

*Worse,* Lucian says. *She leaned closer.*

That last line hangs in the air between us, and I can't tell if it's a warning... or a reminder.

Madison shifts her weight, gaze never leaving mine. "Tonight. Same place we were last time. Midnight."

Before I can respond, she's already walking away, her words settling like iron in my chest.

The apartment feels colder when I step inside, like it's been sitting empty for years instead of hours. I drop my coat on the couch, but I don't sit.

*You know this is a trap, right?* Michael says while pacing.

*I know,* I mutter, crossing over to the bathroom mirror. Talking to them this way has always made me feel a little less crazy.

*Doesn't mean you don't walk into it,* Lucian's tone is deliberate, almost approving.

I brace my hands against the counter, leaning in. My reflection stares back at me — Jace, but with just enough shadow in the eyes to remind me I'm not alone. Somewhere behind that glass, HIM is there too, listening.

*You think she's gonna push again?* I ask.

*She doesn't have to,* Lucian says. *You're already standing on the edge.*

That thought sits heavy in the back of my skull. I push away from the mirror, moving to the bedroom. The dresser drawers feel loud when I pull them open — each shirt, each jacket a decision I don't want to admit matters.

*You're dressing like it's a date,* Michael's tone sharpens.

*It's not a date.*

*Right. It's an invitation to step into whatever game she's playing. Same difference.*

In the corner of my mind, there's a low, steady presence — HIM, silent but impossible to ignore. The kind of silence that waits for an excuse to act.

I pull on a dark shirt, heavy enough to cut the cold, light enough to move in. My boots are worn but solid. By the time I'm ready, the clock on the wall reads 11:02.

Fifty-eight minutes until midnight.

Fifty-eight minutes for HIM to keep pacing.

Fifty-eight minutes for me to decide if I'm going to keep pretending I'm the one in control.

The air outside bites sharper than before, slipping past the collar of my coat as I head toward Penn Station. The streets are half-empty, shadows pooling in the spaces the streetlights don't reach.

*She's going to make you wait again,* Michael mutters.

*I know.*

*She wants you restless. Off balance.*

*Then she's not going to like what she finds,* Lucian cuts in.

The station's South Concourse is exactly as I remember —
fluorescent glare, echoing footsteps, the hum of voices
bouncing off tile and concrete. I pick the same spot by the
pillar, facing the entrances.

11:58.

HIM is close now, not pacing but watching — a pressure at
the back of my skull like a hand resting there.

Then, at 12:00 on the dot, I see her. Moving through the
space like she doesn't notice anyone else, eyes locked on
mine.

*Round two,* Michael says.

*Yeah,* I murmur under my breath. *Let's see what she's really
after.*

She closes the distance without hurry, but every step feels
deliberate, like she's counting them. When she stops, there's

only a breath of space between us.

"You came," she says.

"I said I would."

Her eyes flicker — not surprise, not relief. Just... taking inventory. "Good."

We stand there in the hum of the concourse, neither of us moving. Then she tilts her head slightly. "You've been thinking about that night."

"Trying to," I say.

*You already know the truth,* Lucian murmurs from the shadows of my mind. *You just don't want to see it.*

Madison studies my face like she heard him too. "Do you remember the street?"

I keep my expression still. "You haven't told me yet."

"I'm asking if you remember it."

*Four blocks south after we left Jack's,* Lucian says, his voice so even it makes my pulse skip. *Alley with the broken streetlight. You stepped over someone's shoe on the way out.*

The image flashes in my head — wet pavement, my boot hitting something soft, a pale sneaker lying on its side. My stomach tightens.

*"What else?"* I murmur, not sure if I'm asking her or him.

Madison's gaze narrows. "You just remembered something."

I shake my head slowly. "Pieces."

Madison shifts her weight, watching my reaction. "You're closer than you think," she says quietly.

Closer to what — the truth, or the thing pacing in the dark?

The crowd thins around us as midnight drags into the next minute. Somewhere in the background, a train announcement echoes off the walls.

"You want to tell me why you stayed?" I ask her.

"That depends," she says, and there's the faintest curve at the corner of her mouth. "Do you want the reason... or the real reason?"

The pulse at the base of my skull jumps. HIM stirs, slow and deliberate, like he's listening for the answer.

# The Warmup

The streets are quieter now, shadows stretching long under the orange streetlights.

Madison's words are still moving around in my head, turning over like stones in a current.

*She stayed,* Michael says, his tone low but edged. *That alone should bother you more than it does.*

*It does.* I just don't want to admit it.

*You're thinking about the alley,* Lucian adds, his voice smooth, anchored. *Good. Keep thinking.*

*What's in it?* I murmur.

*Not what,* he says. *Who?*

That lands heavier than I like. My hands curl inside my pockets, knuckles brushing the lining.

By the time I reach my building, I've already made up my mind — no sleep tonight. Not until I've gone over every frame I've got in my head from that night.

Inside, the apartment feels smaller, like the walls are leaning in. I hang my coat, kick off my boots, and drop into the chair by the window. Outside, the street is empty except for a single car crawling past, headlights dragging over the brick.

*If we're going back there, we're going in ready.* I say.

I glance at the clock — 12:47 a.m.

*We will meet her again tomorrow night,* Michael says. *And this time, she's not walking away without giving something up.*

*If that's the case, then we don't need my bleeding heart right now.*

Michael perks up. *Say less, interrogation, my specialty.*

(Michaels pov)

The apartment is quiet except for the faint hum of the fridge and the tick of the wall clock. I'm standing by the window, watching the streetlights burn through the fog outside. The city looks half-asleep. I'm not.

*What's the plan?* Lucian says, leaning forward. *She's too quick on her feet for us to just show up and wing it.*

*You think she'll come armed?* ask.

*Not with a gun,* Lucian says. *With questions. And leverage.*

From the corner of my mind, Jace stirs, his voice even, almost tired. *We keep it in the open. No alleys. No closed doors. The less room for HIM to get dragged out, the better.*

*Oh, there it is,* I mutter, sarcastic. *The 'safety-first' lecture.*

*It's not a lecture,* Jace says. *It's the only way we all walk away breathing.*

Lucian speaks up, voice low and edged with that practiced patience I know won't last. *This isn't my territory. I don't hunt answers. I don't circle suspects.*

*You're part of this.* Jace says flatly.

*I'm part of what happens after,* Lucian replies, his tone cooling further. *You want me in the room for every stare and half-truth, fine. But don't pretend you called me up for conversation.*

*We might need you,* I say. *Not for the usual.*

Lucian doesn't answer right away. When he does, it's sharper. *Then pick a better reason. Or I'll make my own.*

I move away from the window, head for the small dresser in

the corner. The top drawer is a mess — gloves, folded scarves, a couple of knives I haven't touched in months. My fingers skim the steel before pushing it aside.

*Not this time,* Jace says. *We keep it clean.*

*Clean is boring,* I shoot back.

Lucian's voice cuts through like a blade. *Clean keeps the lights on. Dirty keeps the blood warm. Choose.*

The silence after that is heavy enough to press on my ribs. I grab a plain black coat from the hook, check the inside pocket for weight — empty — then slip it on.

*We watch her body language first. Look for the tells. If she's stalling, she's hiding. If she's moving fast, she's scared. Either way, we push.* I say.

Jace adds, *And if HIM starts to wake—*

*—then you step aside,* Lucian interrupts, the finality in his tone leaving no room for reply. *And I'll decide if he stays chained.*

The clock ticks louder somehow.

I stand there for another minute, coat half-zipped, staring at the reflection in the dark window — three sets of eyes behind mine, all of them waiting for different things.

Tomorrow night isn't just another meeting. It's the kind where one wrong move could decide which version of me walks home. And which one doesn't.

I lock the door behind me, the click sounding louder than it should. The hallway smells faintly of old carpet and cold air.

I check the corners like usual. Never trust a hallway this quiet.

Jace's sigh is a low rumble. *It's an apartment building, not a kill zone.*

*That's when you get blindsided,* I snap.

Lucian doesn't bother with words at first — just a faint hum of disinterest. *Then, you're both missing the point. The only thing that matters tonight is the moment she looks at you and decides which one of us she's speaking to.*

We step into the street. The cold hits sharper than it did this morning, like it's been saving itself for this walk. Streetlights throw pale pools of light onto the cracked pavement.

A siren wails somewhere far off — not close enough to matter, but close enough to feel.

HIM moves again, slow and deliberate, like he's keeping pace with my stride but just far enough in the dark that I can't see his face.

I keep my hands in my pockets, coat collar turned up.

*You think she's already there?* Jace asks.

*If she's smart, yeah,* I say. *Scouting the ground, finding her exits.*

Lucian's voice slips through like smoke. *Or maybe she's behind us, watching how you walk. Testing if you're worth meeting at all.*

The thought tightens something in my chest.

We pass under a flickering streetlight. My shadow stretches out ahead of me, too long, too thin. For half a second, it looks like there's more than one.

Jace notices too. *He's closer than I thought.*

*He always is,* Lucian replies.

The city's thinner at this hour. Cars hiss by in the distance. A man in a heavy coat leans against a wall smoking, eyes following me just long enough to make my skin itch.

I catch it immediately. *Three more steps and he'll try too—*

The man looks away. Doesn't move.

*Never mind, false alarm.*

I slow our pace slightly. *We're close enough to see her from here. Keep the approach clean.*

Lucian's voice is quiet now, almost a whisper meant only for me. *If this goes wrong, I'll take it from here. But I won't put him back.*

My steps don't falter, but my pulse does.

I can see the corner up ahead where the streetlight burns steadily and unbroken. That's where I'll see her.

Or she'll see me first.

Her silhouette cuts into the glow of the nearest streetlamp before her face does — that same deliberate stride, that same way of looking through the space between you instead of at you.

I stop, letting her close the distance. She stops just inside arm's reach, coat shifting slightly in the wind.

"You're late"

Her mouth curves like she's deciding whether to apologize or make it worse.

"I wanted to see if you'd wait."

*Don't give her the satisfaction,* Lucian mutters.

"You said you had answers."

Madison's gaze flickers down, then back up, slow enough to feel deliberate. "I do." She tilts her head, studying me like she's listening for something beneath my words. "But the question is... which one of you actually wants them?"

That earns a beat of silence inside. Jace bristles. *She's baiting.*

Lucian speaks, voice calm but edged. *She's not wrong. And she knows exactly where to stick the knife.*

"Start talking."

She takes a step closer, her voice low enough that it's almost swallowed by the wind. "That night... you weren't all here, were you?"

My pulse jumps. Lucian leans in hard. *Ask her what she saw.*

"You're asking the wrong way," she says softly, almost amused. "I'll give you pieces. See if you can put them together."

*She's playing a long hand. But she's circling the truth.* Lucian says.

"Pieces?"

Her smirk deepens. "You were already on edge before you walked into the bar. Someone had been watching you all day. You felt it, but you didn't know who."

I glance at Lucian's shadowy presence in my mind. *That true?*

*More than she realizes,* Lucian says. *But she's leaving out why.*

"What happened next?" I ask.

She lets the question hang a moment too long, then steps just close enough that her coat brushes mine. "You want that answer?" she whispers. "Then I need to talk to the one who did the damage."

That stills all three of us at once. I go quiet. Jace's jaw tightens. And Lucian...

Lucian shifts like a man setting down a glass. *I can give you what you want,* he says evenly. *But you won't like how she reacts when I do.*

The streetlight above us hums, throwing her in that half-light where you can't quite tell if someone's smiling or sizing you up. Madison shifts her weight, one boot scuffing against the pavement, eyes locked on mine like she's about to crack something open.

*She's going to say it,* I mutter, a mix of anticipation and irritation. *I can feel it.*

I keep my face still, but inside, the air feels tighter. Lucian's presence sharpens in the back of my mind, cutting through the noise. *She's about to tell you something I don't want you hearing.*

The words hit like cold water. *Why?* I ask him silently.

*Because some truths don't make you stronger,* he says. *They just drag you under.*

Madison tilts her head, reading me the way she always does — like she knows she's not just talking to one man. "You've been wondering what really happened that night," she says, voice low, almost coaxing.

*Don't bite,* Lucian warns, his tone steady but edged. *You're not ready for it.*

*She's toying with us,* I snapped. *We need to push her. Make her give it up.*

Her eyes flicker — just for a heartbeat — and then she smiles like she's holding something heavy in her pocket and deciding whether to hand it over.

"I could tell you," she says, stepping closer, "but once I do...

there's no taking it back."

Lucian's voice hardens, a quiet command in my skull. *Walk away.*

Her gaze locks with mine, and for the first time tonight, I see it — the exact second she's about to spill. Whatever she's holding back is right there, balanced on the edge of her lips.

I'm already leaning forward, practically vibrating. *She's going to say it, Jace—*

Lucian moves faster than thought. His presence doesn't just rise — it slams forward, flooding every corner of my mind, like a surge of black ice.

The world tilts. My voice cuts off mid-sentence. My consciousness folds inward, muffled like it's been shoved behind thick glass.

(Lucians pov)

"Ahh finally!"

The cold in my chest sharpens into something clean, precise. My breathing slows. Every muscle in my body settles into that deliberate stillness that belongs to me alone.

Madison's lips part like she's about to speak, but I step forward and close the distance before a word can leave her mouth. "Not here," I say, my voice low enough to make her eyes narrow, then flicker with something else. Confusion? No. Recognition.

She tilts her head, studying me. "You're not him."

"No," I say. "And that's exactly why you're coming with me."

Her pulse jumps — I can see it in the hollow of her throat — but she doesn't step back. I turn and start walking. I don't check if she's following. I don't need to.

We start heading to my place. I'm going to get answers tonight. Plus, I need to find out all she knows. I have to keep what happened quiet. They're just not ready to accept the inevitable.

By the time the apartment door clicks shut behind us, the air between us is thick with something far heavier than questions. The need is there — sharp, coiled, and absolute. The urge to dominate, to take every answer she's holding and pull it from her in a way the others never could.

She leans against the wall, one eyebrow raised like she's daring me to make the first move. "You're different," she says.

I take a step closer, slow and measured, my shadow

swallowing hers. "And you're about to find out how much."

I changed my mind, fuck the others. The hours ahead are mine. The questions can wait. Right now, there's only the game I play best — and I don't stop until my partner is ruined and shaking in my hands.

# Ruin

I watch her watch me, that defiant little smirk tugging at the corner of her mouth like she thinks she's the one in control.

She's wrong.

I move without rushing, every step measured, closing the distance until the heat of her breath brushes my jaw. My hand comes up, fingers tracing along her jawline just enough to make her still, my thumb resting under her chin.

"Tonight," I murmur, my voice a controlled blade, "you don't get to run. You don't get to hide behind questions."

Her pulse kicks harder. I can feel it through my fingertips.

"You want answers?" I tilt her chin up until her eyes meet mine. "You'll give me everything first."

There's no more talking after that — just the sound of the air shifting between us as I push her back against the wall, claiming the space, claiming her.

My mouth crashes into hers. My hand wraps around her throat, tightening. She lets out a soft gasp and I swallow it.

My other hand trials up her body, making her eliciting

moans of pure ecstasy.

I've been doing this kind of thing for a while now. Most women are easy to please. They say they want that soft sweet passion but deep down they want to lose control, to lose themselves. If only for a night.

I shift my body to give me better access to her. She's trapped between the wall and myself. Her body arched into mine as my fingers dive into her panties.

I find that little bundle of nerves and start making slow concentric circles. Drawing out moan after moan. It's not long before her nails dig into my shoulder's. Her body trembles with her release.

"That's one down, several more to go." I say with a grin.

She looks at me wide eyed before she speaks. "You're going to ruin me aren't you."

I don't need to answer that, she's said it more of a statement than a question. She knows the answer, plus I hate small talk, especially in the bedroom. Which is exactly where we are headed.

"Clothes off, lay down." She does as she's told, no one can resist when I'm like this.

I move around the bed to pull out the restraints. Placing her wrist in one, I then move around to the other side and secure that wrist. Making sure her arms are pulled tight, I move to the foot of the bed, securing each ankle. Then I leave to get the Mask. My Mask.

The one thing that separates me from all the others. It is me, I am it.

When I return, I can tell she's nervous. She's never done this before. "This is a bit much don't you think?" She says with a slight quiver in her voice.

I don't care what she's saying, I don't respond to her words, I'm watching her body. And it's telling me everything I need to know. She's turned on, begging. Her pussy is drenching my sheets. Plus, she's not fighting and didn't fight me when I put her in restraints.

"It's time you get to know who exactly is in control here." She looks over at me, shocked. She finally registers my mask, and the voice modulator that makes my voice lower than normal.

I make my way back to the bed, slowly, deliberately. Watching as her face lights up with curiosity. I climb up her body like a predator. Cupping one breast I start gently massaging it, running my thumb over the stiffened peak. I pinch her other nipple between my fingers, giving it a light tug.

She struggles against the restraints, moaning and gasping as I continue my onslaught to her breast.

I work my way down to her core, and I can see that tight little bundle of nerves pulsating with need for another release. "Is she really going to be this easy to get off?" I ask out loud. More to myself than anyone.

"Wait!" She shouts, "I haven't showered or shaved today." I let out a low chuckle, ignoring her protest.

One thing about wearing a mask, if you're not precise with your movements it can hinder the moment. Luckily for me I've become a pro.

As I'm lowering my mouth to her sweet little cunt, I slowly push my mask up. Taking her clit into my mouth, I start to feast.

Sucking on her clit at first, just toying with her. She tries to move her hips but it's pointless. The restraints are doing their job. I dip my tongue into her pulsating pussy, tasting her. She tastes like honey dew.

I slip her clit back in my mouth and slowly push my finger

inside her hot cunt. She gasps, letting out a long moan. I proceed to pump my finger in and out while circling her clit with my tongue.

When I add a second finger she bucks. I wrap my free arm around her thigh and place my hand firmly in her abdomen. Gripping her tight and holding her down.

"Now there will be none of that tonight." I say against her pussy.

She moans in protest when I stop pumping my fingers.

"Only good girls get to cum. Control your body."

"I-I'm sorry" she says with a shaky breath. "I'll be good, I promise. Please don't stop."

I go back to eating her out, edging her till I can tell she's panting with the expectation of a release.

I pump my fingers in and out faster, making sure to rub that sweet spot on top during each outward stroke. My thumb circling her clit simultaneously. Her breathing starts to pick up, faster, heavier.

She's close, and I won't deny her this time. I watch as her body starts to spasm. Her hips buck and pussy clenches around my fingers like a vice. I feel her explode. She comes hard. Juices squirting, coating my hand in her cum.

I haven't pulled my fingers out yet. Letting her ride her orgasm out.

After a minute or so, I remove my fingers and tempting as it might be to put them in my mouth and clean 'em off myself, I don't.

I shoved my fingers in her mouth, letting her taste herself. "Clean them." I say, my voice distorted from slipping my mask back in place.

Her eyes roll back as she swirls her tongue around my fingers. Not missing a drop.

She looks at me with those bedroom eyes. The ones that I hate to see. I'm not the person that deserves those, and she's about to find out why.

I get up and retrieve the rope. Setting it aside, I undo the restraints and flip her over. Putting her ass in the air, I get the rope and secure her thighs to her calf's. Pulling her arms back behind her, I use the cuffs I always keep on me and secure them around her wrist.

"Too tight?" I asked. "No." Madison says in a timid little voice. I can tell she's a little scared. I don't care. Not when I can see her pussy still wet with her juices and begging for more. I tighten them a little more till I hear her yelp. "Good girl," I coo.

I bring my face to her pussy and ass that's on display. I run my tongue from her clit all the way to her perfect little puckered hole. I press my thumb in covering the first knuckle. She jumps a little. "Don't worry, I will eventually claim there too." I say with a deep laugh.

Positioning myself at her entrance, I slowly push into her sweet, pulsating core. Inch by inch I can feel her stretching to accommodate my size. I'm just a bit above average. Nothing to boast about. But she is tight.

Once I'm fully seated, I give her a minute to adjust. She's going to need it for what I'm about to do.

I start thrusting, hard. Switching up between fast and long strokes. Her body moving along to the motion. I reach for the cuffs and pull her up just a little. I can hear her cries of pain, and it just fuels the fire.

I reach around and pinch her nipple, rolling it between my fingers. I give it a little tug, and she cries out in pleasure as I feel her pussy grip me tight.

She starts to push back against me when I slow. I need to draw this out a bit longer. I don't get much time when I'm like this. And I like to make it last.

I pick the pace back up. She tries to turn around and look back but I pull her cuffs even harder. "Eyes front!" I tell her.

Doggy style is the best position. I can't stand looking into their eyes.

At the pace I'm going now she won't be able to last much longer. I've already made her cum multiple times. She's panting heavily right now. "I can't cum anymore. Please, no more." she begs. I don't relent. I increase my speed.

Pounding into her tight wet cunt, I can hear her breathing really pick up now. The sounds of our bodies colliding together are a symphony I'll never tire of hearing.

"Just a little longer. Hang in there, you can do this." I try to coax her on.

I release her cuffs and she falls forward. My hand shoots out, wrapping around her throat, dragging her back up to me. Her back is pressed tight against my chest as I keep my grip firm on her throat and lean in to whisper in her ear.

"Did you really think you were in control at all throughout any of this, pet?"

"I-I'm s-sorry" she pants out. "Oh god" she moans.

I give one final thrust and spill inside her as I release her throat and she falls toward the bed. I feel her pussy clench and release a few more times before I slide out.

"Watch what you tell the others, or next time I won't go so easy."

She tries to turn around and look but she's still tied up. Only just now realizing this, she motions for me to untie her. I oblige cause well...I'm not a complete asshole.

After she's released, I grab my med bag and start looking over her body. Scanning for any injuries. I applied a little ointment around her wrist to help with the healing, but I know the ropes I used wouldn't leave any bad marks. Well at least not ones she would hate.

It's been a couple hours since I took control, I can feel 'em waking up. Guess I've got maybe 30 minutes left.

Let's hope she heeds my warning or we're all screwed.

# Residual Heat

It starts as a dull knock on the inside of my skull — faint, then grows sharper.

Jace is the first to stir, his voice dragging itself up from somewhere deep.

*What... the hell... happened?*

I don't answer. I'm busy watching Madison from across the room. She's perched on the edge of the bed, legs crossed, hair messy in a way that looks both deliberate and dangerous.

Michael comes next, his tone tighter. *Jace...? Why are we—*

He stops mid-sentence, probably because he sees what I see — rope marks faint on her wrists, a light sheen of sweat still clinging to her skin, and the fact she's not exactly avoiding my gaze.

It's time for one of them to take back the steering wheel. I'm content, like a wolf in the aftermath of a kill.

*You're welcome.*

(Michaels pov)

Jace's voice spikes in irritation. *You took control.*

*Full control,* Lucian corrects. *Had to. You boys weren't ready for what she was about to spill.*

I push forward, almost growling. *You mean you didn't want us to hear it.*

Madison tilts her head slightly, watching me like she's still in the middle of some private joke. "You're all back now," she says softly. "I can tell."

I try to step forward, but it's sluggish, like wading through wet cement. "What did he do?"

Her smirk widens just enough to feel like a blade. "Which part? The sex? Or the part where he kept your little secret?"

My pulse spikes. "Secret?"

Lucian finally sighs — and it's the kind of sigh that says he's already bored of this conversation. *You'll find out when it's time. Not before.*

Madison rises from the bed, moving slowly. She walks past me, close enough for her shoulder to brush mine. "Midnight tomorrow," she murmurs. "I'll bring the next piece."

The door clicks shut behind her, and I'm left with simmering anger, Jace's suspicion, and the faint, satisfied hum of Lucian in the back of my head.

*You're playing a dangerous game* I say

*Correction,* Lucian replies. *I'm winning it.*

The door's barely shut before the silence swells — the kind that feels heavier than any noise. I don't move at first, just stand there, listening to her footsteps fade down the hall.

Jace is still trying to push forward, voice tight.

*You let her walk out.*

*She wasn't going to talk tonight,* Lucian says, his tone flat, final. *And I wasn't about to waste my time dragging it out of her.*

*You mean you weren't about to waste your fun,* I snap back.

I move to the kitchen, flicking on the light. The clock on the stove reads 3:04 a.m. The glow feels harsh after the dark, and the apartment smells faintly of sweat and rope fiber.

*What exactly happened here tonight?* I ask, even though I already know pieces.

Jace's voice is low. *You saw the marks. You saw her face.*

*Yeah, but I didn't see the part that matters — the part before that.*

Jace hesitates. *Lucian's hiding something.*

*That much is obvious,* I say, pulling a glass from the cabinet and filling it at the sink. The water runs cold, sharper than I expected. I take a slow drink, thinking. *What isn't obvious is why he thinks keeping us in the dark is worth more than whatever game he's playing with her.*

Jace is silent for a beat, then mutters, *Because if we knew... we might not let him out again.*

I set the glass down harder than I meant to. *Then we're going to have to make sure the next time he steps in, we're ready to step right back.*

Jace almost laughs. *Good luck with that. You know what he's like when he wants something.*

*Yeah,* I say glancing toward the bedroom where the sheets are still tangled, the mask tossed carelessly on the floor. *I do.*

The first hint of sunrise presses faint against the blinds, turning the room a dull gray. I have a full day before she's supposed to meet us again. But thinking's not going to be enough this time.

I grab a notebook from the drawer and flip it open on the counter. My handwriting's quick, sharp — habits from when speed mattered more than neatness.

Step one: force her to talk.

Step two: keep Lucian from interfering.

Step three... I hesitate, tapping the pen. Step three is still a blur. Because step three depends on what she says —and on whether I can believe her when she says it.

Jace chimes in again, more cautious this time. *If we push too hard, she might shut down completely. You saw her — she likes being in control of what she reveals.*

*That's exactly why we push,* I answer. *You don't let someone like her set the pace. You set it, or you're chasing her shadow until she disappears.*

There's a long pause before Jace mutters, *You sound like him.*

I don't bother denying it.

*Because maybe, to beat Lucian in his own game, we'll have to borrow some of his rules.*

◉

The apartment still smells faintly of her — perfume and sweat tangled in the air like smoke after a fire.

Jace is still simmering from what Lucian pulled, and he's in no shape to lead.

He's pacing somewhere in the background of my head, muttering about boundaries.

*We should wait until midnight,* he says.

*"That's exactly why we're not,"* I mutter aloud.

Lucian gives a low, amused hum. *Curiosity's gonna chew you up, Michael.*

I ignore him.

The plan's simple — find her before she finds us. Throw her off balance. See what slips.

It's not about confrontation. Not yet. It's about pressure in the right spots.

I dress down — jeans, dark hoodie, nothing that screams interrogation.

Coffee in hand, I step out into the cold morning air, letting the city wake around me.

She'll be out there somewhere, moving like she's in control.

My jobs to remind her she's not.

"Michael?"

I stop mid-step.

Jack's standing there, hands jammed in his coat pockets, eyes squinting against the wind. He looks like he hasn't slept either, but his grin is the kind that says he's got something I need.

"Wasn't expecting to see you out here," he says.

I keep my tone casual. "Looking for someone."

He tilts his head. "Madison?"

I don't answer right away. Jace stirs in the back of my skull, already suspicious. *How the hell does he know?*

Lucian just chuckles. *Because he's part of it.*

Jack's grin widens like he heard that. "She's good at finding trouble. You should know — you've been in it together before."

I step closer, just enough to make him shift his weight. "What do you know?"

He shrugs, but it's too slow to be innocent. "Enough to tell you you're not the only one she's been talking to about...

that night."

The words land heavier than they should.

Jace's pulse spikes in my chest. *Ask him what he means.*

I don't. Not yet.

Instead, I let a slow smile creep in. "Then you and I need to have a real conversation, Jack."

Jack glances past me, scanning the street like he's expecting someone else to walk up.

"She's not the only one you should be watching," he says, voice dropping low. "You've got more than one problem breathing down your neck."

Jack takes a step back, hands still deep in his pockets, eyes never leaving mine.

"You can run after her," he says, "or you can hear what I've got to say. But you can't do both right now."

Jace's voice is sharp in my head. *We find Madison — she's the one holding the cards.*

Lucian is quieter, but colder. *Jack knows something you're not ready to hear from her mouth. If she says it, it'll hit harder.*

Jack seems to read the hesitation. "Tick-tock, Michael."

He nods down the street. "I'll be in that diner for the next fifteen minutes. After that..." he shrugs, "I disappear."

I glance toward the corner where Madison usually cuts through when she's in this part of the city. No sign of her yet, but if I go into that diner, I'm giving her up for now.

Jace pushes again. *She's the priority.*

Lucian finally breaks the stalemate. *The priority is not getting blindsided, idiot.*

Jack starts walking toward the diner, slow like he knows I'll follow.

The wind cuts sharper now, and for a second, I'm just standing there — caught between chasing the woman who knows the truth and the man who might burn me with it first.

Fuck it.

The bell above the door gives a lazy jingle as I step inside. The diner's heat slaps me in the face, thick with coffee and fried bacon. Jack doesn't bother looking back — just slides into a booth at the far end, away from the windows.

I dropped into the seat across from him, the vinyl creaking

under my weight.

"You have ten minutes now." I say.

Jack signals the waitress without even glancing at me. "Black coffee, two sugars," he tells her. Then, to me, "You want anything?"

Jace mutters in my head. *Cut the small talk. Make him say it.*

"I'm fine," I say flatly.

Jack leans forward, forearms on the table. "You think she's playing you?"

Lucian's voice slides in like smoke. *He's not here to ask questions. He's here to feed you something.*

"What's your point?" I ask.

His grin doesn't touch his eyes. "My point is... you weren't the only one with her that night."

Jace's pulse spikes instantly. *What does he mean by that?*

I keep my voice steady. "Say it straight, Jack."

He takes a sip from the mug the waitress just set down, stalling. When he speaks again, his tone drops to something darker.

"Someone else walked her home. Someone who wasn't you... and who doesn't like you very much."

Jack stirs his coffee lazily, like we've got all the time in the world. "Thing about a night like that," he says, "is people remember it differently. You remember pieces. She remembers pieces. And then there are the pieces nobody talks about."

Jace's voice is sharp in my head. *He's stalling.*

I lean forward. "And you just happen to have those missing pieces?"

Jack shrugs. "Maybe. Or maybe I just know where to look."

The diner hums around us — forks scraping plates, a couple arguing softly in the next booth — but it's all white noise. Jack's watching me like a man measuring rope for a noose.

Lucian cuts in, low and bored. *He likes the sound of his own voice. Let him talk. He'll hang himself.*

"You weren't the last one with her," Jack says finally. "You left. She didn't."

Jace pushes forward hard. *Who?*

Jack smiles into his coffee, takes another slow sip, then sets the mug down with a soft clink. "Midnight came... and he was already there. Waiting for her."

I grip the edge of the table. "Who was there?"

Jack leans back, studying me for a long moment. Then he drops it like a stone in still water.

"Your old friend... HIM."

The word punches through me. My spine stiffens.

I start to lean forward. "Jack—" I never finish the sentence.

A crushing weight slams down, like someone just dropped the ceiling onto my skull. My ears ring. The edges of the diner blur.

Then I feel it.

The sudden, vicious yank from inside — HIM doesn't crawl or sneak his way in. He claims. One violent motion, and Jace is gone. I vanished right after, dragged under by an invisible undertow.

Lucian tries to dig in, voice sharp and vicious, but he's slammed into silence.

I'm locked in the back seat now, staring through my own eyes while HIM takes the wheel.

The air in the booth thickens. My breathing slows.

Shoulders roll forward. Chin dips. My hand — HIS hand — flexes once against the table, slow and deliberate.

Jack's face changes instantly. Not just pale — bloodless. His lips part like he's about to speak, but nothing comes out. His pupil's quake in his skull.

HIM doesn't say a word. He doesn't have to.

He just stares. And in the space between us, that silence is deafening.

Somewhere far away, dishes clink. A waitress laughs softly with another customer. But here, inside this booth, the sound dies before it reaches us.

The pressure ratchets higher until my vision whites out at the edges. Then—

It snaps.

Lucian tears upward, colliding with me as we force HIM down, locking him somewhere deep.

The aftermath hits like a wave. My body sags, palms flat on the table, breath coming in hard bursts. My fingers tremble against the sticky laminate.

*Jace,* my voice comes in tight, urgent. *Breathe.*

Jace's voice is just a raw whisper. *I can't...*

I force in one ragged breath, then another, feeling each one scrape against my ribs.

Jack's still staring at me — eyes wide, chest heaving, frozen like prey that's seen the shadow of the predator pass over it.

# Fall-Out

The cold night air slaps my face the second we push out the diner door, the bell above it still jingling behind us.

*We can't stay here*, Lucian mutters from somewhere behind my eyes. *Too many people. Too many eyes that might've seen.*

Jace doesn't say much — not that he could. He's there, but it's like trying to talk through a mouth full of water. Every step feels heavier for him. HIM's brief grip left him wrung out, pale and shaky in the back of our mind.

*Eyes up*, Lucian presses. *She's here. I can feel it.*

I scan the street — doorways, alleys, the gaps between parked cars — every place Madison could melt into. The city hum is muted, every passing stranger a blur.

*She wouldn't have stuck around after that*, I say under my breath, but it's more for me than them.

*You're wrong*, Lucian replies, calm, certain. *She's curious now. People like her never walk away without pulling at the thread.*

I left, cutting down a side street that smells faintly of smoke and wet concrete. *If she's hiding, she picked the wrong night.*

We move quickly — not running, but with that pace that makes people instinctively step aside. A man in a long coat glance, hesitates, and then keeps moving.

*There*, Lucian says suddenly. *Third building, recessed doorway.*

I catch the faint outline of a figure half in shadow. Shoulders hunched, head tilted slightly — like she's watching us, but not enough to be obvious.

*Told you*, Lucian says.

Jace's voice finally drifts up, hoarse, tired. *If we're doing this... you lead. I'm not...*His words break off, the weight in them obvious.

*We know*, Lucian says, quieter now. *Just rest.*

I focus on that doorway, steps carrying me toward her, the city noise dimming to nothing but the sound of our boots on pavement.

And Madison doesn't move. She just waits.

The distance closes slowly, deliberately. Not because we can't get there faster, but because none of us are ready for what she's about to say.

"You took your time," she says, voice low.

"You didn't run," I say, matching her tone.

Her lips twitch like she's holding back a smile. "Would've been pointless."

*She knows,* Lucian murmurs, and the certainty in his voice grates.

Jace stays quiet in the back, but I can feel him watching, straining past the exhaustion.

Madison pushes off the doorway, closing the gap until she's just a breath away. "You want answers," she says. "But you're not ready for all of them."

"Then start with one we can handle." I snap.

Her gaze flicks over my shoulder, scanning the empty street like she's making sure we're alone. "That night... you weren't just your normal four."

Jace's pulse kicks hard, and I feel Lucian stiffen.

"What the hell does that mean?"

Madison's answer comes slow, deliberate — each word landing like a drop of ice water.

"It means," she says, leaning in just enough for her breath to touch my ear, "there's another."

The words slide in like a blade, slow and cold. Jace stiffens immediately.

Lucian doesn't speak right away — which is worse. When he finally does, his voice is measured.

*Careful, Michael.*

I force my expression to stay flat, though my grip on the moment is tightening. "You're gonna explain that."

Madison's eyes don't waver. "Maybe I will. But if I do, you're not going to like what you hear."

"Try me."

Her smirk sharpens. "The other......doesn't sleep. Does not wait. He doesn't care about your rules, your order." She glances down the street, then back at me. "He's the reason you're all still breathing. And the reason you might not be much longer."

Jace's voice cracks through, shaky. *She's talking about HIM.*

*She can't be. She said four earlier. That's you, I, Lucian, and HIM*

Lucian finally cuts in, his tone low, deliberate. *End this conversation. Now.*

*"Why?"* I mutter under my breath.

*Because if you keep her talking,* he says, *he's going to hear.*

For a fraction of a second, the air changes — colder, heavier, like the street just lost all its sound. My muscles lock without my permission.

Madison notices. Her gaze flicks between my eyes like she's seeing who's looking out from behind them. "He's here, isn't he?" she whispers.

Jace's panic spikes. *Get her out of here!!!!*

I don't move. The pressure's building again — heavy, suffocating — crawling up from my gut into my chest. The air between us feels electric, every second stretching too long.

*Michael,* Lucian warns, voice clipped. *You need to step back.*

*I'm not—*

*Now.*

It's too late. The break comes like a lightning strike — sudden, violent. My voice is ripped away mid-breath, leaving only silence where he was. My muscles lock tight.

My jaw grinds. My pulse is no longer mine.

And HIM is here.

He steps forward without hesitation, and the world narrows to the space between him and Madison. His voice is a low growl, thick enough to rattle the bones.

"You weren't supposed to see."

But instead of fear... she smiles.

Slow, deliberate, like she's been waiting for this. Like the sight of him isn't a nightmare, but the answer to some deep, buried hunger.

"You are not who I was talking about." She coos at him. "But it's really nice to finally meet the one all the others fear."

HIM freezes mid-step. That reaction — not fear, not panic — stops him.

She lifts her hand slowly, the way you'd approach a wild animal, and lays her palm against his cheek. Her thumb strokes once, gently. "Ssshhh," she murmurs, smiling wider.

The fury bleeding through HIM's muscles falters. His breathing slows, deepens. The storm behind his eyes doesn't vanish — but it focuses, sharp and unwavering, entirely on her.

Lucian's voice slips through like a breath of cold air. *What the hell is this?*

HIM doesn't answer. His head tilts slightly into her touch, the anger melting into something heavier... darker.

Then, just as suddenly, he steps back.

Control snaps to me like a whip. Jace is gone — drained completely — leaving only the two of us conscious here.

Madison lowers her hand, still smiling like she's just unwrapped the gift she's wanted for years. Without another word, she turns and slips into the shadows.

The night air rushes back in, sharp and cold, but I'm not breathing right. Lucian's voice is quiet now.

*We need to talk about this.*

*I'm not sure I want to.* I say, somewhat in control.

# Regroup

The cold sits on my shoulders like a wet coat I can't shake.
Neon flickers over puddles, taxi's hiss past, and the last trace
of Madison's perfume thins into the night until there's
nothing left but the echo of her smile and the way HIM
leaned into her palm like a loaded gun deciding not to fire.

*We're not chasing her,* I say. My voice comes out steady. It's
supposed to.

*Agreed,* Lucian answers, flat as iron. *We're done for tonight.*

Jace doesn't answer. He's not even a murmur. Just the
blank, dreamless weight of someone who fell through the
floor.

I tug my coat tighter and start walking. Not fast. Not slow.
That pace that opens a path through late-night traffic and
the tail end of bar crowds. People don't know why they
move for me, they just do.

*You saw that?* I ask the dark, because it's not like I'm asking
the street. *She didn't flinch. She wasn't afraid.*

*She called him,* Lucian says. *Not with words. With nerve.
And familiarity.*

*Familiarity,* I repeat, tasting the word like it might bite back. *It means she's done this before.*

*Means she thinks she can do it again.*

*Can she?*

Lucian doesn't answer, which is an answer.

We cut west two blocks to bleed into thinner streets—brick, dumpsters, a grocery's steel shutter that looks like it's been punched by a god. A subway grate exhales steam in quick, exhausted breaths. Somewhere, a delivery truck backs up and beeps like a metronome that learned menace.

*I hate how quiet he is,* I mutter.

*He'll wake after he gets some rest,* Lucian says. *Or when he smells coffee.*

*Coffee I can do.*

We hit seventh and hang south, past a pawn shop window full of guitars that never got famous and rings that never made it back onto fingers. A bike messenger ghosts by, chin tucked, his scarf a flag of surrender. I keep my eyes moving—corners, doorways, rooflines. HIM is down again, but the mind doesn't forget the shape of his shadow right away. It takes a few blocks for the nerves to stop bracing for the second blow.

*He was angry,* Lucian says after a while. *Not the usual... surge. Focused. Directed.*

*Directed at her,* I say.

*At the fact, she knew him.*

*We'll split hairs later. Right now, we get home.* I roll my shoulders. *And we keep our face straight if anyone calls our name.*

We don't make it half a block before somebody does.

"Hey! Michael!"

I don't turn. Not until I place the voice and the rhythm under it—the gravel, the warmth, the way it hangs on a word like it wants a little company there. Joe.

He's got the endcap of a sidewalk staked out like a pulpit— milk crate for a stand, cardboard hand-lettered sign propped against it. The sign's been taped and retaped so many times the tape is practically architecture. A dented thermos steams by his boot. Tonight, he's in the army coat with the missing button. Knit cap, beard gone saintly white around the edges. The city calls him a street preacher; I call him a compass that still points north, even when the magnet gets petty.

Jace likes him. He never rushes past, always buys the coffee and listens to the stories and leaves with pockets lighter and heart heavier in the good way. Which is hilarious, because Joe talks like thunder and Jace prefers rain.

"Evening, Joe," I say, and Lucian shifts in the back—*Keep moving*—but I ignore him and stop.

Joe's eyes crease. "Evenin' nothing. It's tomorrow already." He taps his watch as if the city might apologize. "You moving too fast, son."

"Story of my life."

He tilts his head, the way he does when he's about to read what you didn't say. The sermon cadence smooths out, lowers. The crowd that hadn't gathered fails to gather. It's just me and him and the soft animal city watching from the corners.

"You look thin in the soul," Joe says. "Thin in the sleep. You tell me why?"

I could tell him. I could say: Because the thing we keep buried found daylight and the woman we don't understand smiled at it like a homecoming. But Joe doesn't deal in nouns, he deals in weather. So, I talk weather.

"Storm front came through," I say. "Didn't break anything.

Just... rattled the windows."

Joe lifts a hand like he's blessing the image. "Storm that rattles without breaking is a warning storm. Says, 'board up or batten down.'" His eyes go to mine, and for a second I feel seen all the way to where the floor drops out. "Where's your quiet one?"

My jaw works. "Under."

Joe nods like that's a place on a map. "You give him rest. Even iron needs a fire and a good hammer to be useful. Miss the fire, you get brittle." His gaze flicks past my shoulder, over my head, through me. "And you... you bring a lot of heat, boy. Careful you don't become the hammer and forget the hands that hold it."

*He knows too much*, Lucian mutters, not accusing— observing.

*He knows just enough*, I snap back, then to Joe, "You still doing late service out here?"

He chuckles. "City sleeps in slices. I preach to the slices that won't."

"Anybody listen?"

"Anybody always does." He leans closer—just enough that

his breath carries peppermint and cheap diner coffee. His voice drops to confessional quiet. "Seen your shadow walking ahead of you tonight. The big one. The one that makes dogs go silent."

The air in my lungs goes narrow. "How close?"

"Close enough to fog the glass." His smile is kind, and I want to punch it and thank it, and both of those are proof I'm tired. "But the glass didn't break. Means the frame's holding."

He pats the sign—THE WOLF IS ONLY A MONSTER UNTIL YOU LEARN ITS NAME—then sees me see it and huffs. "Don't get cute, boy. You're not a t-shirt." He nudges the thermos toward me. "Drink. You tremble like a wire."

I take it because Jace would. The coffee is black and honest. Jace stirs for the first time—a small curl of steam under a door—then subsides. "Thanks."

"You tell Jace," Joe says, hitting the name like he always does, careful and respectful, "I like him best when he walks slow. World will ask him to hurry towards everything that hurts. He can say no and still be a good man."

"He knows," I say, and my voice cracks at the end, which

annoys me. "We're headed home."

Joe's eyes soften at home. "You need bread?"

"We need quiet."

"Take both," he says. He slings the canvas bag from the crate's far side and palms a wrapped loaf like a magician makes a dove appear. "Warm. From DeMarco's. Tell your bones they're not alone in there."

I tuck it under my arm. "Preaching to the slices again."

"Always." He tips two fingers against his forehead, and mockingly salutes me. "Walk easy, Michael."

I turn to go. He calls after me the way prophets do when they pretend they're not: "When a hand calms a beast, it's not always mercy. Sometimes it's ownership. You make sure it's the right hand."

A little static runs through my chest. *He saw more than we wanted*, Lucian says.

*Everybody sees more than we want*, I answer. *Tonight, they just said it out loud.*

We move. I don't look back. Joe's voice slides up into a sermon-beat behind us, threading with traffic, turning the corner of the block into a kind of chapel.

"—and I tell you, city of teeth and bright eyes, there walk among you men with whole forests inside them, and if you call a wolf, you better know its name—"

The rhythm carries us south and east, then the words are brick again, and the brick is ours.

I shoulder the apartment door and it sticks like it always does in winter, and I love it for being stubborn in familiar ways. The deadbolt complains when it turns. The radiator knocks like a neighbor you half-like. The room smells like soap and winter and us.

# Mindscape

*(Michael's POV)*

I set the bread on the counter and don't take my coat off, not yet. The quiet lands hard.

*We are not talking about how she touched him*, I say. *Not until he's up. Then we talk once, slow, and nobody screams.*

*I don't scream*, Lucian says, almost offended.

*I do*, I say. *So help me out.*

I dump keys into the bowl, miss, hear them skitter under the chair, leave them there. Shoes off, finally. The floor is cold enough to reset a man. I cross over to the window, check the glass out of habit. Faces reflected, the city doubled, my posture saying too much. I close the curtains a third of the way and stop; I like the sliver of night like a lookout slot. I drop down into the chair, close my eyes and let myself drift back.

*I look around the apartment and almost laugh. Figured my*

*mind couldn't be bothered to come up with anything original.*
*The so-called "mental map" looks exactly like the real place.*
*Same counters, same curtains, same chipped bowl by the door.*
*Real creative, Michael. I guess even in my head, imagination*
*takes the night off.*

Where do you want him? *Lucian asks.*

The bed.

*Lucian places Jace down on the couch instead,* Promise you
won't fucking go back out.

Not going out, *I say, and for once I mean it.*

*We move as one in small ordinary ways. Tap on. Glass filled.*
*Two Advil rattled from a bottle. Coat finally off, hung on the*
*chairback that it always slides off. I pull Jace forward the way*
*you coax someone out of a heavy sleep. He stumbles and I catch*
*him without hands.*

Hey. *I say, and for once the word is soft enough to surprise me.*

*He doesn't answer, but he leans. I walk us to the bedroom. The*
*sheets are a little crooked. I set the Advil on the nightstand*
*and the water beside it, and I sit on the edge of the bed until I*
*feel his breathing even out. It takes longer than it should.*

He's out again, *Lucian says, less annoyed than he sounds*

*about most things. Good.*

*I stand, but the room sways a little, so I sit again. My hands
are still faintly shaking. I study them like they belong to a
man who made worse choices than I did. Then I laugh once,
humorless.* You think Joe's wrong?

About ownership? *Lucian considers.* I think a hand that
calms without fear has a history. Or a plan.

Both can be true, *I say.* Which one scares you more?

The one that makes him lean.

Yeah. *I scrub my palms over my face.* That's the one.

The apartment fills up with heat in uneven, radiated
breaths. The building settles–the city sighs–a siren tells a
joke two streets over that I don't get. When the first edge of
dawn thinks about the horizon, the gray in here shifts
shades.

I get up and move to the kitchen because kitchens are where
problems feel smaller—the way clatter cuts through
thought. I slice the bread Joe gave us, warm it in the oven,
watch butter surrender into it like an argument deciding it's

not worth the time. The smell loosens something tight in my chest.

I eat standing, because chairs feel like commitment.

*Halfway through the second slice, Lucian speaks again.*

She said there's another.

I heard her.

And then she smiled at him like she'd made a wish and it worked. *He replies.*

I saw that.

Don't pretend this is just curiosity.

I'm not pretending anything. *I set the plate down too hard, hearing it complain.* I'm prioritizing. He wakes first. Then we set rules. Then we decide if we call her, or she calls us.

She'll call us. *Lucian says, a little too confident.*

I know. *I stared at the door, at the lock, at the small scuff from the last time I kicked it on a bad day.* And when she does, we'll answer.

We answer as who?

Me, *I say.* I'll take it.

He won't like that.

He doesn't have to.

And if the big guy answers first?

*I breathe slowly.* Then we make sure the hand on his cheek is ours.

*Lucian lets the quiet sit again. Not sulking. Not retreating. Just... waiting. He hates long conversations, and this counts. Eventually, the radiator knocks in a rhythm that almost sounds like applause from another room.*

Hey, *I say to the quiet, to the room, to the part of me that's all elbows and jokes and quick hands and bad ideas made good by timing.* We're not broken.

Not yet, *Lucian replies.*

*The city outside decides to try morning. A truck coughs awake. A bus sighs and kneels for nobody. The upstairs neighbor drags a chair two inches like they owe the building proof of life. I look at the phone and don't pick it up.*

*Jace hasn't moved, but his breathing is steady now. He's still a little pale. HIM's double appearance drained him in a way that isn't physical, more of mental break.*

*I'm at the window, one hand on the curtain, peering out at the street below without really looking at anything. My mind's running faster than my eyes.*

We can't keep going like this, *I mutter.*

We'll keep going however we must, *Lucian replies, the tone low but certain.* You saw her. She's not running. That means she's not done.

*I glance over his shoulder toward the bedroom door.* Jace's got nothing left in him right now. If something happens—

Then we keep him out of it until he's ready.

The sound of the coffee pot finishing up brings me back out of the mindscape. I pour the black liquid in a mug, the steam rising in soft spirals. The smell of coffee fills the air, almost enough to pretend this is just an ordinary night.

I turn fully now, leaning against the wall. *She said there's another. That's not nothing.*

*It's worse than nothing,* Lucian says. *It's a hole in the floor and we're already falling through it.*

Silence stretches, broken only by the faint creak of the

apartment settling.

*We wait,* I say, *We let him rest. We get our bearings. We leave when we have to.*

And when we leave, *Lucian adds,* we'll be ready.

I start to pace the living room, the worn boards creaking under each step. I don't like standing still, not when the city outside hums with a thousand moving pieces I can't see.

I sit at the kitchen table, coffee cooling in my hands.

*You're burning energy you'll need later,* Lucian says, watching my restless loop.

*I'm burning time,* I mutter back. *Time that could be used to track her.*

*Patience.* Lucian says with that cocky demeanor.

*How long before Jace is back on his feet?* I ask.

*Depends. HIM hit him harder than either of us expected.*

A soft scrape draws my attention to the wall by the window. I cross the room and press my ear to it. *Pipes?*

*Footsteps,* Lucian corrects. *Two floors up. Someone's moving slow.*

I stayed there, listening. The sound comes again, measured, deliberate. Then silence.

The urge to move, to check it out, gnaws at me. But leaving now would mean dragging Jace into the open. Not happening.

I set my coffee down and pulled the blinds open an inch. The street is mostly empty, save for a stray cat darting under a parked car. Streetlight glare turns the pavement slick gold.

*She's out there somewhere,* Lucian says. *Watching.*

I step back from the wall and exhale. *Then she'll have to wait. We're not walking into another ambush.*

We spend the next hours in that uneasy rhythm, Lucian's voice threading through my thoughts, and me pacing, checking locks, testing the front door chain twice.

Jace stirs once, mumbling something we can't make out, then slips back under.

When the first streaks of pale gray light touch the edges of the blinds, the air in the room shifts. Not colder—heavier. Like something leaning against the walls from outside.

I freeze mid-step. *You feel that?*

*Yes.* Lucian replies.

It's not a knock. Not a voice. Just... presence.

We don't know if it's her, or something worse. But whatever it is, it's waiting. The weight outside doesn't go away. It lingers, pressing against the building like it's trying to seep through the brick. I move first, silent toward the peephole. Nothing. Just the dim hall light buzzing and the warped green carpet beyond the door. It is impossible to relax, I take a step back and grab the baseball bat leaning in the corner.

*Not smart,* Lucian warns. *If it's who I think it is, a bat's not going to matter.*

I grip it anyway. *Then it's for the other kind of trouble.*

A faint sound—barely a breath—comes from the other side of the door. Not a knock, not footsteps. Just... someone there.

Jace stirs. *Who...?* His voice is weak, still wrapped in exhaustion.

*Shh* I call quietly.

*Huh?* Jace says.

Oh wait, right, in the head.

The sound outside changes—a single scrape, metal on metal. The doorknob turns half an inch before stopping. The pressure against the walls eases... then vanishes entirely.

For a long moment, none of us moved. I slowly open the door. The halls are empty.

*We're not leaving until we have to.* I say.

*We need to act fast when we do,* Lucian says.

The quiet hangs heavy, the kind that settles into the drywall and makes you second-guess every creak. Jace hasn't moved, but he's awake now and his eyes look glassy, skin pale. HIM's double appearance still has him dragging.

I pace near the couch, blinds still shut, every so often I check the street through the narrow gap between the slats. Nothing. Then the burner phone on the counter buzzes. Once. Twice. Three times. I snatch it up before Jace can even protest. Lucian hums low in the back of our mind, interested.

On the screen: Madison.

No words in the text—just an address and a time.

She doesn't wait long, *Lucian says.*

I stare at the phone for a beat, jaw tight. *She picked the pier.*

*That's out in the open,* Jace says hoarsely. *Too exposed.*

*Which means she's either got a plan,* Lucian says, *or we're walking straight into someone else's.*

I pocketed the phone. *We're going.*

I can feel Jace try to move in behind the wheel but he's still too weak.

*I guess you're taking the lead Michael.* He says.

*That's the point, you're not ready. Rest up.*

Lucian chuckles, low and knowing. *Oh, this should be fun.*

# The Tide Turns

*(Michael's pov)*

The city feels different when you know you're being summoned.

Streetlights seem sharper, alleyways deeper.

Lucian keeps to the background, murmuring here and there, like a coiled spring waiting to be let loose. Jace's presence is faint, a shadow behind closed doors, conserving what little strength he's regained.

The pier is only ten blocks away, but it feels longer. Every step clicks against the damp pavement, echoing off shuttered storefronts.

*You feel that?*

*Oh, I feel it*, Lucian says, slow, almost savoring it. *Like static before a storm.*

Traffic thins the closer we get, until the streets open wide and empty. Out here, the smell of salt rides the air. Gulls wheel overhead, their calls sharp in the dark.

At the third block, a man steps out from a recessed

doorway. Thin frame, patched coat, eyes bright and fevered.
Joe.

"Evenin', brothers," he says, voice rising and falling like a
sermon half-remembered. "The waters are restless tonight.
Something's coming in with the tide."

I slow, narrowing my eyes. "You always talk in riddles, Joe?"

He smiles without warmth. "Only when the truth is too
heavy to hand over all at once." His gaze flicks over my
shoulder — no, through me — like he's counting who's
inside. His smile fades. "Not all of you made it here tonight,
I see."

*He sees more than he should,* Lucian murmurs.

Joe's voice drops. "Don't keep her waiting. The tide turns
fast." He steps back into the shadows without another
word.

The pier comes into view ahead — black water shifting
under pale light, the faint silhouette of a lone figure leaning
against the railing.

Madison. Waiting.

Jace is still weak, though he's managed to surface a little.
*This place... it's too open.* His voice is faint, like wind over an

empty bottle.

*That's why we're here,* I mutter, mostly to myself. *No walls. No corners. No surprises.*

We make our way to Madison. Stopping short when we see a look of frustration on her face.

"Why the sour face?" I say

Madison looks like I just kicked her puppy. Damn what I wouldn't do to keep that look off her.

"Why can he never be the one I meet first? It's always you or Jace, never the other one." She says

"Well to be quite honest," I start "he isn't' for everyday adventures. He exists due to a very traumatic event that came before I or Lucian. Jace can tell you. He is without a doubt, our last line of defense."

She's still pouting. "I want to talk with him."

"He doesn't exactly make hou—" My words are cut off. I'm thrown back into my mind. Mentally slamming into Lucian, while I see a look of excitement through my eyes.

No, his eyes. He did it again. HIM is out. Talking with Madison. I scan for Jace and find him laid out. *Well, you held out as long as you could. Lucian, a little help here?*

**(HIM's pov)**

Why do I always come when she calls? I hate coming out. This world is nothing but pain, suffering and heartache.

Heartache from people that are meant to love you. Meant to care for you and tell you everything is fine.

*Hey big guy, what's the deal?* I hear Lucian say.

*ENOUGH!!!!!!* I scream back. *Tell the others to give me five, and I'll be done, and tell Jace I said sorry, I never mean to hurt him.*

*He knows,* Lucian says.

I turn to Madison, my posture unlike the others, and definitely not like that other one. He's very new. But familiar in a way.

"I'm here, little one."

"Yes, you are." she says, with a look that stirs something in me.

"Why do you keep asking for me? I'm not meant for this world. I only hurt, that's what I was made for." I say, my head trying to look anywhere but those damn sun kissed eyes of hers.

"You were made for so much more than what you believe, but right now I just want to look at you." she says as she reaches for my face and turns my head, locking eyes with me.

"I want to say thank you.... you know, for that night."

"The others wouldn't have been able to handle that guy, and to be honest...I....it...never mind."

I say looking away.

"Can the others hear or see us right now?" she asks

"No, I've locked them out."

"Wow, so Lucian can take control every now and then, and you're able to do that and lock them out?" she asks with a smile on her face,

"Don't get any ideas"

She straightened up, her face worrisome now.

"I know about the other guy." she says

"And? I barely know about him. That night was his first appearance, and I don't much like him anyways, and if you are asking if the others know, they don't. Well aside from Lucian. The others aren't ready though." I tell her.

"I need him. If he was strong enough to take over all of you, then I need that guy."

"Too bad" I say. I can feel myself getting worked up. The anger, feeling like an old friend. The power surges through me. I see Madison reach up and cup my cheek. Everything stops; calm overtakes me.

"Just a few more minutes please?" she says with a voice like a siren, calling to all the pirates and fishermen. Is that what she's going to do? Lead us to our death?

"Ok, then I need your help. The guys from the other night are still out there. Watching, probably right now. Can you help me?"

"You don't need me. You need the Strategist."

"Lucian?" she asks.

A deep laugh rises from me out of nowhere. "Heavens no, Michael is who you need. It's why he's always present when you meet us. He is analytical, cold, strategic, and decisive. When things in our life don't start to add up, he's the one Jace runs too. That's why he was made."

She blushes now, I'm assuming from remembering exactly why Lucian was made.

"How much longer do you have?" she asks. I understand what she's hinting at, but it can't happen tonight.

"Not tonight, and not long left, I knocked the main one out when I came forward. If the others don't take over soon its needles and doctors for the next week or two."

"Oh, ok" she says with a sad expression creeping over her face.

"Soon," I say, "but for now I will relay what you want. And in the future, ask for the Strategist."

"Michael?" She says his name like a question.

"Yes, goodbye for now, little one." I say walking away towards an all night diner.

Now I can finally get some rest. Although the others think I'm always trying to break free. I just want to protect him, that's why I'm here. Whatever.

As I'm walking, I get that feeling again. The same presence from that night. The other one. When was there a need for someone like him?

He's just watching.

*Okay okay, I'm giving up control.* I say to any of them. I don't really care who. As long as Jace is safe, that's all that matters.

I'm a few paces from the front of the diner when I'm mentally yanked back and I see Michael being flung forward, but he looks out of it.

*What-The-Fuck?*

# 3 Coffees And A Warning

*(Michael's pov)*

The café is nearly empty at this hour, the kind of place that survives on night owls and people who'd rather hide than sleep.

A single ceiling fan turns lazily above us, pushing the smell of burnt espresso and sugar through the air.

Last thing I remember is HIM taking over and Jace being laid out, and now I'm here? What is happening?

I claimed the booth in the far corner, sliding in with my back to the wall. Lucian doesn't argue — it's the kind of position we both prefer.

Jace's still dead weight in the passenger seat of our headspace, his presence faint and uneven, like static on a bad radio signal.

The waitress shuffles over, looking like she'd rather be anywhere else. "What'll it be?"

"Three coffees," I say before she can pull her notepad. "Black. Hot. Fast."

Her brow furrows, just for a second, like she's about to

make a joke — but something in my tone makes her shut it and walk away without another word.

*You think caffeine's gonna fix him?* Lucian asks, leaning back, arms folded. Like he's actually sitting.

*It's better than nothing,* I mutter, scanning the windows. *I need him at least half-awake before tomorrow.*

Lucian smirks faintly. *Before her.*

The coffee arrives in mismatched mugs, the steam curling up between us like ghost breath. I set one in front of Jace's usual seat — a gesture more than anything — before taking a long pull from my own.

Inside, Jace stirs, weak and groggy. *What... where...*

*Drink,* I say, tilting the cup just enough for the smell to hit. *We don't have much time.*

*Time for what?* Jace's voice is faint, but there's a flicker of awareness now.

Lucian leans forward, the edge of a grin cutting across his face. *Time to decide if you're ready to meet her again — or ready to keep HIM locked in when she comes calling.*

I don't let the silence last long. I start tapping the side of my mug with one finger, a steady rhythm that sounds like thinking.

Jace sips slowly, leaning forward on his elbows. His color's coming back — not much, but enough to lose that half-dead look.

*You're here now,* I say, watching him over the rim of his cup. *Good. I was about five minutes from throwing cold water on your face.* Metaphorically of course.

*Wouldn't be the worst thing you've done to me,* Jace mutters, still groggy, but getting sharper.

Lucian exhales through his nose, unimpressed. *You two done with the reunion? I'm only here because none of you know how to handle her if things turn... intimate.*

Jace shoots him a look. *You mean violent.*

Lucian grins faintly. *Same difference.*

The coffee shop hums softly — low jazz over the speakers, the occasional clink of a mug against ceramic. Outside, the streetlights buzz like tired sentries.

For the next hour, we trade quiet conversation.

Little things. Not plans, not warnings — just talk.

I tell Jace about a half-finished novel the guy at the counter is pretending to write. Jace tells me about a customer from two years ago who tried to order "water without the wet." Lucian barely listens, only stirring when Madison's name drifts into the conversation.

Finally, the clock behind the register clicks over to something that feels late enough to call it a night.

I toss a few bills on the table and slide out of the booth. *We're going home.*

The walk back is unremarkable — no shadows that move wrong, no voices whispering from alleyways. By the time we hit the apartment door, the adrenaline from earlier is gone, replaced with the heavy drag of exhaustion.

Inside, we don't talk much. Jace collapses on the bed without even taking his shoes off. I claim the armchair by the window, eyes half-lidded but still watching the dark outside. Lucian fades to the back, content to let sleep claim us all.

For a few hours, at least, the apartment is quiet.

*(Jace's pov)*
The apartment is still, the kind of stillness that doesn't quite feel natural. A pale wash of morning light spills through the half-closed blinds, cutting the room into sharp bars of gold

and shadow.

The air has that faint overnight chill, quiet enough to hear the tick of the clock in the kitchen — slow, steady, too steady.

It's not the light that wakes me. Not the cold either. It's that other thing. The weight.

Not heavy like sleep, not heavy like exhaustion. Heavy like someone is leaning over the bed, not touching me, just close enough that the air bends differently. It's there before I open my eyes. It's there when I do.

The ceiling swims into focus above me. Michael stirs somewhere inside, muttering half-formed thoughts. Lucian isn't saying a word — which is somehow worse than his usual disinterest.

I swallow, slow. *You feel that too?*

Michael shifts, tension pulling his voice taut. *Yeah. He's here.*

Lucian finally speaks, voice low, almost lazy. *Told you he wouldn't stay quiet for long.*

I turn his head toward the corner of the room — the one that's somehow darker than the rest, even with sunlight creeping in. Nothing moves there. Nothing blinks. But the air's thicker in that spot, like the shadow itself is breathing.

I push myself upright, the sheets sliding down my chest. My heart isn't hammering — not yet — but every beat feels measured, deliberate. Like my own body is pacing itself for what's coming.

I keep my eyes fixed on that darker corner. *"I know you're there,"* I say quietly, the morning rasp in my voice roughening the words.

No answer. Just that slow press of presence, the air still bending around something I can't see.

I breathe deep, steadying myself. *"You've been quiet... longer than I expected. I don't want this to be a fight. I just—"* I pause, swallowing hard, *"—I just want to understand."*

Michael shifts uneasily in our head. *Careful, Jace.*

*"I need to know why you keep coming,"* I continue, voice low but even. *"What do you want? From me? From us? HIM, talk to us."*

The silence stretches — long enough that I wonder if I'm just talking out loud to nothing. Then, just as I draw a breath to speak again, it happens.

The corner shifts. Not a movement exactly, more like a slow, deliberate turn of attention. The weight in the room sharpens, every hair on my arms rising. And then, a single word.

"Her."

Michael is first to speak. *What'd he say?*

*Nothing,* I lie. My voice feels too small.

Lucian gives a short, humorless laugh from the back of the mind. *That wasn't nothing. I felt it roll through you.*

*I said it's nothing,* I snap, sharper than I meant to. My palms are damp, fingers curling into fists against the sheets.

Dragging my hand down my face, I school my features. *We're fine.*

*Bullshit,* Michael says, but he doesn't press.

Lucian just hums like someone who already knows the punchline. *Suit yourself.*

The apartment is still — the hum of the fridge, faint traffic below, sunlight creeping along the floorboards — but none of it reaches me the way it should. My ears are tuned to that one word still rattling in my chest.

Her–Madison.

I throw my legs over the side of the bed, feet hitting the cool wood.

*I'm getting coffee,* I mutter.

*You just woke up,* Michael says.

Yeah. And I'm staying awake.

I start the coffee pot as soon as I enter the kitchen. Lucian starts to drift forward just enough to murmur, *you know you can't keep it from us forever.*

I stare at the swirling steam rising up from the pot, jaw tight. *Maybe not forever, but long enough.*

The silence that follows isn't agreement — it's just patience. The kind that waits for cracks to spread.

The coffee is bitter, too hot, the first swallow burns, but it's exactly what I need.

*You're jumpy,* Michael says. *You don't usually flinch at shadows.*

I don't answer. Leaning against the counter lost in thought, I watch a line of dust twist lazily in the sunlight cutting through the blinds.

Lucian stirs, his tone lighter but still edged. *You think if you ignore it, it'll go away? You heard him. You know what that means.*

My fingers tighten around the mug. *I'm not having this conversation.*

*You will,* Lucian says simply. *When she's standing in front of us again.*

The mention of Madison twists something low in my stomach — not quite fear, not quite anticipation. I set the mug down, a little too hard. Ceramic clinks against the counter top.

They don't talk after that. The apartment settles into a low hum, the kind of silence that isn't really silent at all. Outside, a siren wails and fades. Somewhere below, someone slams a car door.

But underneath it, I feel HIM — quiet now, resting. Not gone. But underneath that, there's something else there. Familiar and foreign. Like a relative you've yet to meet, but when you see them it's like you've known them the whole time.

I shake it off, I've got to focus.

By late morning, the coffee's gone stale in the bottom of my mug. I rinse it out, the motions slow.

*We're not going to look for her today,* I say, though no one asked.

Michael grunts in mild protest. *Why not?*

*Because,* I say, drying the mug and setting it back in its place, *sometimes the bait comes to you.*

The knock comes just after noon — not loud, not hurried. Three even taps.

I freeze halfway between the counter and the couch. Michael immediately bristles. *We're not expecting anyone.*

Lucian's tone sharpens. *Don't open it.*

Ignoring them both, I step towards the door. I haven't undone the chain, not yet. Cracking the door, I see one pale eye peering back at me from a weathered face. A man — late thirties maybe, hair plastered flat from the rain — doesn't smile, doesn't even blink.

"You Jace?"

I hesitate. "Who's asking?"

The man reaches into his jacket. I tense like I'm about to throw the door shut, but the guy only pulls out a folded scrap of paper and holds it out to me.

"From a friend," the man says. His voice is flat, without any hint of accent. "Said you'd know."

"What's your name?" I say reaching for the paper.

The man just shakes his head. "I'm just a courier."

Then he's gone, already turning down the hall, footsteps fading like he was never there.

I shut the door. The paper feels heavier than it should.

*Open it,* Michael urges.

Just two words, scrawled in a familiar hand: Midnight. Pier.

The air in the room tightens. I don't have to turn to know HIM is awake again, the weight of that attention pressing in from every shadow.

Lucian breaks the silence. *Looks like the bait came after all.*

I stare at the paper. Hoping that if I stare long enough, it will disappear.

Michael paces toward inside, arms crossed. *We're not doing this.*

I fold the paper. *You don't even know what this is And you wanted to go looking for her earlier.*

*I don't need to,* Michael shoots back. It's her. *She's nothing but trouble, and after last time—*

*After last time? You mean after HIM came out?* Lucian cuts in, his voice lazy but edged. *Because let's be real... that's what you're scared of.*

I can feel Michael staring at Lucian inside. *No. I'm scared of what happens when we give her the chance to pull us in deeper.*

Dropping into the chair I let out a big sigh, *You feel it though. Same as me.*

*Of course we feel it,* Lucian says. *It's like gravity. And gravity doesn't care if you think it's a bad idea.*

Michael shakes his head. *We walk away now, we can still breathe tomorrow. We go down there...* He trails off, jaw tight.

My fingers tap the folded note. *She's not going to stop, you know. She'll just find another way to get close.*

*Which could be worse,* Lucian adds, like he's enjoying fanning the flames.

Michael glares at him. *Or she'll give up. People give up when you don't feed them.*

*Do you believe that?* I ask.

Michael doesn't answer.

We sit in the stale quiet for a beat too long. The rain outside has turned steady, the sound of it wrapping the room in a kind of hush.

Finally, Lucian chuckles low. *You can lie to yourself all you want. But you'll be at that pier.*

I exhale slowly. *We've got twelve hours to decide.*

*There's no decision,* Lucian says. *Only delay.*

The hours drag. I plant myself at the small table with a half-read book, eyes sliding over the words without absorbing a single one. Michael camps on the couch inside our mind, remote in hand, flipping channels like maybe the right image will erase the thought of her.

*Pathetic,* Lucian says a little after three, his tone like he's lounging somewhere with a drink in hand. *You're both pretending to live your lives while counting down in your heads.*

I snap the book shut. *Shut up.*

*To me? Or to yourself?* Lucian chuckles.

Michael doesn't look up from the TV. *Ignore him.*

The smell of rain drifts in through the cracked window. Somewhere a siren wails, long and low, before fading into the city's hum.

I try the book again, but every time my eyes skim a paragraph, a different image forces itself in — Madison's smirk, the way she looked when she said there's another, the heat in her voice when she'd stood too close.

Michael sighs, leans back, and changes the channel again. *We could be using this time to figure out what the hell she meant. Or why HIM nearly tears through the seams anytime she's around.*

*Or,* Lucian drawls, *you could admit you liked seeing her touch him. Like seeing her calm him down when none of us could.*

*That's not the point,* Michael says sharply.

*That's exactly the point.*

The rain gets heavier, steady percussion on the windows. I finally toss the book aside, get up, and start pacing.

Michael watches me for a moment. *You're thinking about going.* He say's more as a statement.

I stop pacing, but don't deny it. *Are you telling me not to?*

Michael doesn't answer right away. Just turns back to the TV and mutes it.

In the silence, Lucian laughs softly. *See? Delay, not decision.*

By nightfall, the apartment feels smaller. The shadows in the corners are longer now, stretching toward them every time the streetlights flicker outside. The rain hasn't stopped, only softened into a thin, steady drizzle — the kind that soaks you before you realize it.

I stand at the window, hands shoved into my pockets, staring at the slick reflections on the street below. Michael hasn't said a word in hours, the muted TV painting his face in flashes of blue and gray.

*It's getting late,* Lucian says, voice a thread of smoke curling through the air. *If you're going, you go now.*

*We're not*—I start, but I'm interrupted my Michael.

*Yeah. We are.*

Our eyes meet for a beat, and that's all it takes. No plan, no debate. Just the shared, unspoken truth that we're already in motion.

I grab my jacket. Michael subconsciously checks the street from the window.

*You boys are too predictable,* Lucian mutters, but there's no fight in it — only a low, satisfied hum.

I step into the hallway, locking the door behind me. The air outside is damp and cold, the drizzle clinging to my hair and shoulders as I start down the street.

And somewhere ahead — whether at the pier or in the dark between streetlamps — she's waiting.

# What She Saw

*(Jace's pov)*

The wind comes in off the water, cutting through my jacket as we close the distance to her.

She's right where Lucian said she'd be — leaning against the railing, eyes fixed on the dark line of the horizon.

Without meaning to, I slow. Something's wrong. It's not the setting — the pier's almost empty — it's the way the air feels heavy, like there's a storm building somewhere deep inside us.

*He's moving,* Michael mutters. *Trying to push through.*

Lucian's voice comes low and flat. *Not tonight.*

The pressure spikes — HIM surging forward, the edges of our vision going sharp. For a heartbeat, I feel myself sliding backward in my own mind, the familiar grip of HIM's hunger wrapping around my throat. It's always hard to breathe right before he takes control.

And then — nothing.

The weight is still there, but it's... locked in place. Held.

Not by Michael. Not even Lucian.

*Enough,* a voice says from somewhere deeper than any of us have reached before. It isn't loud. It doesn't need to be. HIM freezes like a chain's been yanked tight.

My breath starts coming back again, but my pulse hasn't slowed. *What the hell was that?*

*Later,* Lucian says.

We're close enough now that Madison finally turns her head. Her gaze sweeps over us, lingering just a little too long, like she's taking stock of all four at once.

And then — she smiles. Not at me. Not at Michael. Not even at Lucian.

Straight through us, to whatever just kept HIM caged.

*Could she perceive all that?* I mutter.

Michael speaks up. *Possibly? At this point, I'm just along for the ride.*

*Let's just get this over with.* Lucian snaps.

She turns away and starts walking toward the far end of the pier, the boards groaning under her boots. I follow — not too close, not too far. The night is cold enough to make my breath visible, and hers drifts back toward me in slow, pale clouds.

I stay quiet, but Michael can't help himself. *She's been holding out,* he says. More so trying to guess at this point. Like trying to hit a bullseye, but you're blind.

We keep moving, gulls crying overhead, water slapping the pilings below. Streetlights along the pier flicker in the wind, casting her in brief shadows of gold.

I finally speak, my voice low. "Why not tell me?"

"Because," she says, stepping up onto the next railing post and balancing for a moment like it's nothing, "you weren't ready. Still might not be."

*She's baiting you,* Lucian warns.

I ignore him. "And now?"

Her balance is perfect as she walks the length of the post and hops down without breaking stride. "Now you're asking the wrong question."

I keep pace beside her, boots knocking against loose boards. "And what's the right one?" I ask.

She stops walking. Turns and looks at me for a long beat before answering. "Why am I still here?"

I shift, but don't answer. Michael keeps his gaze locked on her, jaw set.

*Don't bite,* Lucian mutters, but it's clear she's already got her hooks in.

Madison turns and starts walking again, slower this time, like she's giving me the chance to decide whether I'll follow. I do.

"You could have left a dozen times," I say. "We've given you plenty of reasons to run."

She laughs, soft but sharp. "Oh, I thought about it. More than once. But every time I got far enough away... something kept pulling me back."

My voice is shaky. "Us?"

She glances at me — a flick of her eyes, a curve of her lips. "Not exactly."

The boards beneath our feet groan under the weight of the pause that follows. Somewhere out on the water, a buoy bell tolls once, then fades.

"Then what?" I press.

Madison's steps slow until she stops completely, leaning against the railing with the ocean stretching black and endless behind her. "I've met people like you before. One or two. But never all at once. Never... together."

I cross his arms. "We're not a party trick."

Her smile is sharp. "Are you sure about that?"

*She's dangerous,* Lucian says. *The more you give her, the more she'll use.*

Madison's gaze flickers to the side — not to me, not to Michael, but inward, as if she can feel the rest of us. "One of you hates me. One of you wants me. And one of you..." she trails off, eyes narrowing slightly, "...would burn the world to keep me."

My chest tightens. "You don't know what you're talking about."

"Oh, I do," she says, turning fully toward us now. "Because I've seen it."

The wind gusts hard, whipping her hair across her face, but she doesn't move to push it back. "That night, you all think I was scared. I wasn't. I was waiting. And for one second..." she leans forward, her voice lowering to a near whisper, "...you were exactly what I've been looking for."

*Walk away,* Lucian urges. *Now.*

But I don't move. The pull she talked about earlier. It's thrumming in our bones, deep and undeniable.

She smiles like she knows it. "That's why I'm still here."

The gulls scream overhead as she turns away from the railing and starts walking toward the far end of the pier. I follow without speaking at first, boots thudding against weathered planks. The moon hangs low, casting silver over her hair.

"You're quieter than I expected," she says over her shoulder.

I clear my throat. "Not much to say. You've... seen a lot of us already."

*Yeah,* Michael mutters. *And you're the last card in the deck.*

Lucian scoffs. *Cards are replaceable. He's not.*

Madison slows until we're side by side. "That night... I had a taste of something dangerous." She looks right at me now, holding all of my attention. "Then I had something darker." Her smile tugs. "But I haven't had you."

My chest tightens. "Maybe you haven't asked."

"I'm asking now."

The air between us thickens. Somewhere deep, HIM stirs — a slow, low rumble like thunder over hills — and just as quickly, the pressure vanishes, cut off mid-growl. That other thing from moments ago has spoken, without words.

Madison notices. Her eyes glint. "It's just you in there now, isn't it?"

I nod. "If you want me, you get me. Nothing else."

"Good." She steps in, her hand brushing his. "Then come with me."

She leads us down the pier, past a shuttered bait shop, out to the street where the lamps hum with moths circling the glass. We don't rush. Her knuckles graze my hand every few steps, a constant reminder of her choice.

The hotel is only a block away — a narrow building of brick and glass, its sign buzzing faintly. The lobby is small, the carpet worn but clean. She doesn't go to the desk. She already has a key.

The elevator ride is quiet. Her perfume swirls in the warm air between us — something faintly spiced, like cinnamon and smoke.

Room 512. She slides the card in, the green light flashes, and she pushes the door open.

I stop in the threshold, looking at her — really looking.

"You're sure?"

Madison's smile softens, but her eyes stay locked on mine. "I've been sure since that night."

I step inside. The door clicks shut behind us.

# Madison

The lock clicks, and for a moment I let the silence settle between us.

Jace stands just inside my door, taking in the room like he's memorizing it — the dim lamplight, the bed, the curtains drawn tight. He's cautious. Careful. That's what I came here for tonight.

I stay where I am, leaning against the wall, and watch him. He doesn't realize how much he gives away just by standing still. Every shift of his shoulders, every measured breath — all of it telling me how close the others are beneath his skin.

"You look like you're waiting for permission," I say.

His eyes flick to mine. "Just making sure this isn't... about them."

I let the smallest smile curve my lips. He needs to believe this is just about him — and in a way, it is. "No. This is about you. Only you."

Finally, one of them mutters from somewhere inside him. I can't hear the words so much as feel them, like a distant echo. Another voice follows, sharper, amused. I imagine it's something along the lines of: *Don't screw it up, pretty boy.*

I don't break my gaze as I step closer, slow enough for him to notice how deliberate it is. He doesn't back away — good. My hand finds his chest, right over the heartbeat that thuds a little harder when I touch him.

"I want to see what's underneath all that control," I murmur. "Not the hunger. Not the dominance. Just... you."

He draws in a slow breath, fingers brushing along my jaw like he's memorizing the shape of me. It's softer than I expected — gentler.

"Better." I whisper, leaning into his touch.

Somewhere deep inside, he stirs — the one I've been aching to see again. HIM, that's what they call him. The air shifts when he moves, the weight of him rolling toward the surface. But just as quickly, he's pulled back. Not by Jace. Not by the others. By that other presence. The one from the pier.

Jace's thumb grazes my cheek. "You're not afraid of what's in here?"

I let my smile widen, but only a little. "Afraid? I've been waiting for this."

I take his hand in mine, lacing our fingers, and give a gentle tug toward the bed. No rush. No demand. Just an unspoken promise in the space between each step.

He doesn't resist, but he doesn't hurry either — like he's memorizing the weight of each moment.

I like that.

At the edge of the bed, I turn to face him, keeping our hands linked as I lean back just enough to pull him into my space. The heat between us blooms in the quiet, the kind that doesn't need a spark — it's already been burning.

Jace's gaze roams over me, not hurried, not greedy. It's intentional, like he's reading a language only I speak. And the way he looks at me makes me want to keep talking in it.

I freed one hand from his, sliding it up the line of his chest, feeling the slow, solid rise and fall under my palm. He covers my hand with his, holding it there for a beat, as if to anchor us both.

"You're not like him," I murmur, voice low, almost swallowed by the quiet.

He doesn't ask who I mean. He doesn't need to.

I step closer until there's nothing between us but breath.

The air thickens, and I can feel his restraint, that controlled edge that's just starting to fray. I want to see how far it goes before it breaks.

Tilting my head, I press a kiss to the corner of his mouth — not taking more than that, just letting the contact linger, letting him feel what's waiting if he follows. My hand slides to the back of his neck, fingers brushing the hair there, and I feel the shiver run through him.

"You're still holding back," I whisper against his skin. "I can feel it."

His hands find my waist, slow but certain, pulling me just enough that the last inch between us vanishes. The shift in him is subtle, but it's there — the decision made.

I smile against his lips, because I already know what comes next.

His breath hitches — almost imperceptible — before his hands tighten at my waist, grounding me in the moment. There's a weight in his touch now, an unspoken shift from possibility to certainty.

The kiss deepens, not rushed, but with an edge that wasn't there a heartbeat ago. His fingers trace along the curve of my hip, lingering like he's mapping every inch for later.

I press closer, feeling the way his chest rises against mine, the warmth of him seeping into me until the rest of the pier, the night, the city — all of it — is just gone.

When he finally breaks the kiss, it's only far enough to rest his forehead against mine, his voice low, almost a growl.

"Tell me you want this."

The words hit like a spark to tinder — and the look in his eyes tells me he already knows my answer.

"Yes" I say without hesitation.

He kisses me like a man possessed. The backs of my knees hit the bed and we fall. He turns us at the last minute, and I'm straddling him now.

He's gentle but firm. I feel his hands roaming over my body. One hand grabs my waist, the other tangles in my long auburn hair.

He fists it, giving it a little tug. A moan escapes my lips. That smirk of his appearing. Showing me that dimple. It's cute.

He pulls me closer, our mouths meeting again. I feel the kiss deepen. Feel his tongue slide against my lips asking for permission.

He's definitely not like Lucian, he takes. Jace is gentle,

loving, kind, and caring. I like him just as much as the
others.

I give in, letting his tongue explore, as does mine. He tastes
like coffee cakes. Cinnamon with sugar. Sweet with the taste
of his favorite coffee. I'll never get enough of him.

I'm so lost in his taste I don't even recognize that I've started
grinding my hips on him.

God he feels amazing. I know we sorta just hooked up the
other day but he feels different than Lucian.

My god just the outline of him is rubbing me in all the right
ways.

I start moaning as I continue to grind my hips against his
erection. My breathing picks up. Faster now, my hips are in
sync with him. Rocking back and forth.

SMACK!!!

I jump a little. Did he just spank my ass?

"Again" I mumble, a little out of breath. He does it again,
and again. Each time feeling better than the last. I need a
little pain to get off.

I'm almost there and he isn't even inside me.

I go to get off of him to further this along but his hand grips my waist.

"Stay, I want to see you please yourself" Jace stares at me with only a look he could give. One that promises forever.

I continue rocking back and forth. I throw my head back, my hair falling down my back. He reaches up with the hand that was on my ass and gives it a little tug. Just what I needed.

I'm about to cum when his hand grips my throat, a little tighter than I'm used to.

"Eyes on me."

He says with that cold voice. I half think it's one of the others, but I can see it in his eyes. And I know it's Jace. My Jace.

I stare at him, never breaking eye contact as I continue to rub myself on him.

"Like this?" I ask.

"Yes, keep going"

"Yes...god yes...you feel so good." I say in a whimper. His hand tightens a little more and I suck in as much air as possible.

"More, yes yes yes" I scream as I cum so hard my vision blurs.

He's still staring at me, smiling. Also basically holding me up by my throat. If he let go I'd fall forward on to him.

In a move faster than I expected he flips us over and pins me down. He starts to kiss me, then moves down my body. Taking off my shirt first and then my skirt and panties. I rarely wear a bra.

He starts to remove his clothes. That's when I notice the scar over his heart. He turns around to set his clothes off to the side along with mine. I notice the matching scar on his back. He turns back around holding his shirt to his chest.

"You weren't supposed to see that. I got caught up in the moment." He says.

"No, it's ok. We don't have to talk about it if you don't want to." I say softly. "Come here."

He moves hesitantly. Then speaks, "He wouldn't let me finish the job"

I shush him. "I don't need to know right now, it's ok. Just be here, with me, for tonight?"

He seems relieved.

He lays me down, and we start making out. His lips start to explore my body.

He kisses my neck, then trails kisses down to my breast. His fingers find the hardened peak of one and gives it a little squeeze while he sucks the other into his mouth.

I start to pant. This man is skilled. And I get a little jealous at the thought of him with someone else.

That's soon replaced with another heavy breath from me as his hands dips down and he starts playing with my clit.

I grip the sheets and clench my teeth as he moves down my body. Leaving kisses on my stomach and hips till he reaches my pussy.

He starts licking and sucking. He grazes his teeth over my clit, eliciting more squeals and moans of pleasure from me.

My hand finds his long dark hair and I grip it tight. Holding him there.

"Please, don't stop. Yes, right there." I moan. "OH CHRIST!!!! YES, DON'T STOP!!! PLEASE, PLEASE, PLEASE!!!!!!"

What the fuck am I begging for? Who fucking cares right now.

"YES JACE!!! OOOHHHH MY FUCKING......JACE!!!!!

I scream his name as my orgasm rips through me. Blinding light accompanies the wave of euphoria I feel as I ride it out.

He rides it out with me. His tongue and fingers gently stroking my clit and pussy.

I look down, I see his sky-blue eyes staring back up at me. "You're even more beautiful when you make your O face." He says with a smirk. I smile back at him.

I pull him up and flip us back over. Both of us naked, I take him in my hands. Stroking him a few times. He's big, I'm not sure I could fit all of him in my mouth. He notices and grabs my hands.

"Tonight's about you. Don't think you have to reciprocate." He says.

I was going to but now that he's said that, it feels like a weight's been lifted. So instead I climb back up and situate him at my entrance.

Last time it was Lucian, and he barely gave me time to adjust. This time I'm taking it slow.

I slip the head in and gasp. He can see the shock on my face.

"Why do you feel bigger?" I ask

"There's no physical difference between us. We're all the same. But it could have something to do with the emotions you're feeling right now. Just take your time." He replies.

I slip him in a little more, inch by inch. He's gotta be at least 9 inches. I can feel him in my stomach.

I lean back a little and look down. Sure enough he's actually showing in my lower abdomen.

I lean back forward after adjusting and start to slowly bounce up and down on this gorgeous man. I place one hand on his six pack and the other on his chest.

I can feel my third orgasm already building. His hand grips my hips. I start rocking back and forth. It doesn't matter what I do at this point. Any movement sends shocks of pleasure through me. His dick hits just right. Pulse's just right Hell it even throbs along with my movements.

I can't take it anymore, I lean forward and kiss him. As I devour his mouth I continue to pump my hips.

I pull away slightly, just to where our foreheads are touching.

Looking into his eyes, those beautiful starburst eyes, I say the only thing I can think of.

"I Love You" ·

He doesn't miss a beat, "I Love You Too"

Staying there I just start repeating it like it's my mantra.
Saying it in time with the up and down and back and forth
of my hips.

I start going harder and faster. Chasing the orgasm I know is
coming.

I slam my mouth to his one last time and kiss him deep as
we cum together. I can feel him spill inside me. I crave that
feeling. Of being full.

I stayed there for what feels like hours but was only about
15 minutes, laying on his chest as he strokes my hair.

"Did you mean it?" He says.

I know what he's talking about without having to ask my
own question.

"Only every time I said it, what about you?"

He looks down and smiles. "I wouldn't have asked if I
didn't mean it...babe."

He said it like he was testing the water. I give in. "Babe....? I
like that. Babe" I give him a smile back.

I sit up and move to get off him. "We better get dressed. I'm sure the others are just itching to talk by now."

He doesn't argue and starts to get dressed. I notice the scars again and stop him before he pulls his shirt back on.

"When you're ready..." I kiss the front scar "I'm ready to listen." I turn him around and kiss the back scar.

"Some time soon." He says with a look that has him lost in thought.

We finish getting ready. Stepping out into the hallway, I turn and lock my door, and we start to head back out to the pier.

# Shadows On The Water

*(Jace's pov)*

The lock clicks behind us, and I follow her into the hallway. She's close enough that I can still feel the heat from her skin, the ghost of her breath against my mouth. My hand finds hers like it's the most natural thing in the world, fingers intertwining, the rhythm of her steps falling in with mine.

We take the long route toward the pier. I'm not rushing this. The air carries salt and the faint burn of frying oil from a food truck closing. Wood planks shift under our weight, gulls calling overhead. It's quiet enough that I can hear her breathing steadily, but with a softness I didn't expect after the way she just let me in.

She leans on the railing when we pass under a pool of lamplight, hair catching gold at the edges. I watch her, not in the way a man watches a woman he wants, I've already had her, but in the way a man watches something he doesn't quite understand yet and doesn't want to miss a single detail of.

"You're not going to ask?" she says without looking at me.

"Ask what?" I already know, but I want to hear her say it.

"Why I'm here. What I'm running from. Who I'm running from."

That's the moment I could push — but I know the cost of forcing someone to open a door before they're ready. "You'll tell me when you're ready."

She laughs, short and almost fond. "Straightforward... but still cautious. Figures."

We keep moving, our footsteps settling into a shared pace again.

Halfway down the pier, a gust comes off the water, sharp and cold enough to lift the hair at the back of my neck. That's when I feel it — the same shift in the air I caught the night I first saw her. Most people wouldn't notice. I do.

I tighten my grip on her hand without thinking. She notices, but her voice is light when she says, "It's fine. Not tonight."

"Madison—" I start, but she cuts me off with a look.

"Later." And that's final.

At the end of the pier, we find a bench. She sits, and I follow, brushing our shoulders. I let my eyes settle on the dark line of the horizon, the rhythmic push and pull of the tide. She's quiet beside me, but I can feel the unease in her posture — the same way I can feel the warmth of her body even without touching.

I don't press her. I just sit there, watching the water, and wait for the night to decide what it wants from us next.

The wind shifts again, colder this time, carrying the faint tang of diesel from a boat farther out. She glances over her shoulder, just for a second — too quick for most people to notice, but not me.

That's when I catch it.

A shape moving at the far end of the pier. Could be nothing. But the way her spine straightens tells me she doesn't think so.

"You see something?" I ask.

Her mouth tips in a smile that doesn't reach her eyes. "Just thought I did."

The words are casual, but inside, I feel them. That subtle twitch in the back of my mind. The quiet sound of someone shifting in a chair.

*You felt that too?* Michael's voice is low and curious.

*Yeah.* I say

Lucian doesn't speak, but the pressure of his attention is like weight on my shoulders — leaning in, listening.

I keep my tone even. "And?"

"And... it's nothing." She looks back toward the water, but her hand tightens slightly on mine.

Not nothing. I let it go for now. Pushing won't get me answers — not tonight. Still, the air between us feels different now. That easy warmth we carried from her hotel is still there, but underneath it... there's a ripple.

We start walking again until the pier's edge forces us to stop. She leans against the railing, staring out at the black water, and I take a step closer, close enough that our arms touch. I let her have her silence, even while the others shift restlessly inside me.

This isn't the moment to go hunting for the truth.

It's the moment to make sure she knows I'll still be standing here when she's ready to give it.

The pier fades behind us, wood planks giving way to cracked sidewalks. Her hand is still in mine, warm, but there's a tension in her arm now — the kind that says she's listening for more than just my footsteps.

*I don't point it out. Not yet.* Michael says.

The streets are quiet, the kind of quiet that makes every passing car sound too loud. Neon spills from a block ahead, buzzing pink and blue against the damp pavement. We pass a diner, the kind with greasy coffee and a jukebox that hasn't worked since the '80s.

"You hungry?" I ask.

She glances at me, then at the neon sign. "Starving actually."

We don't rush. Just fall into step, boots scuffing the sidewalk. The smell of fried food hits us before we're through the door. Warm air, bacon grease, and coffee — it wraps around us like a blanket.

A waitress with tired eyes and a name tag that says Louise points us to a booth in the back. She drops off menus we probably won't look at.

Madison slides into the seat across from me, stretching her legs out until her boots bump mine under the table. She smirks. "You ever going to ask, or just keep dancing around it?"

My brows lift. "Ask what?"

She leans back, the corner of her mouth twitching. "Exactly."

Inside, Michael perks up, amused. *She's baiting you, man.*

Lucian's silence is heavier, waiting, assessing.

I studied her for a moment, but she's already reaching for the coffee pot Louise left on the table, pouring herself a cup like nothing happened.

She takes her first sip of coffee like she's got all night. I can tell she's enjoying watching me sit in this silence — the kind she's not going to break first.

Inside, Michael stirs. His voice is clearer now, closer to the surface.

*Alright, man... enough pussyfootin'. You're not gonna ask, I will.*

I blink once, keeping my eyes on her. She doesn't know he's here, not really, but sometimes it feels like she can hear him anyway.

*Don't give me that look,* Michael goes on. *You've been circling her for days. She drops that breadcrumb? You think I'm letting that slide? Nah. We're getting answers tonight.*

Lucian's voice rumbles faint in the background, more of a warning growl than a word.

Michael ignores him. *You can keep playing safe, or you can let me drive. You know I'll get her talking.*

My fingers tap once against the coffee cup. Madison tilts her head, eyes narrowing slightly — not suspicious, just reading me like she always does.

"Something on your mind?" she asks.

More than she knows.

*Say the word*, Michael urges. *And I'll get you what you're too damn polite to ask.*

The hum of the diner fades into the background. My jaw tightens. She's still watching me — waiting, maybe even hoping I'll take the bait.

And I'm starting to think Michael might be right.

The diner's half-empty, all chrome and neon, smelling like burnt coffee and syrup that's been sitting too long. The kind of place that feels untouched by time.

Madison's across from me, her fingers wrapped around a mug, steam curling up into her hair. She's relaxed — or she wants me to think she is. Every now and then her eyes flick toward the window, like she's checking the shadows outside.

Inside, Michael stirs.

*She's not just checking shadows, man. She's checking for something. Someone.*

I ignore him. "You want anything else? Pie? Fries?"

She smirks. "You trying to feed me or avoid asking what you really want to know?"

"You did say you were starving."

That gets a quiet chuckle from Michael. *See? She already knows you're stalling.*

Lucian rumbles in the background, low and irritated, but Michael just leans into it.

*Alright, you've danced enough. Let me drive.*

*"No,"* I mutter under my breath.

Madison tilts her head. Eyebrows pulling together forming a crease between them. "No... what?"

*She's baiting you. Perfect. I'm taking this,* Michael says, and before I can stop him, he's right there, in my voice, my body. Damn you, Michael.

*(Michael's pov)*

My shoulders loosen. I lean back in the booth like I've owned this spot for years. "Nah, I'm just done watching you dodge me. You've been leaving crumbs since the pier. I'm ready for the damn loaf."

Ah, there it is. That little flash in her eyes when the tone shifts — surprise mixed with curiosity. She wasn't expecting Jace to grow a spine this fast, which tells me she still hasn't figured out she's not talking to him anymore.

Her fingers pause on the rim of the mug, her body language doing that push-pull thing. One part wants to bolt; the other part wants to lean in.

"Oh, so we're doing this now?" she says, eyebrows lifting just enough to look playful — but I can smell the tension underneath.

"Yeah," I tell her, settling deeper into the seat like I've got all night. "Now. Unless you want me to wait until the others are listening. I promise I'll be a lot less gentle then."

Her lips press together, and I can see the wheels turning. She knows what's coming if she stays quiet — but she's also smart enough to realize I'll get it out of her eventually. Might as well be here, in this booth, before the rest of the peanut gallery chimes in.

"That night…" she starts, her voice dropping half a register, "…wasn't random."

I lean forward just enough to make her feel the gravity. "Didn't think it was. Who?"

She glances at her coffee like it's going to save her, then shakes her head. "If I tell you, you'll start a war you can't win."

That gets a dark little laugh out of Lucian somewhere in the background, but I keep my gaze locked on her.

"If they're hunting you," I say, slow and steady, "they've already started the war. I'm just deciding when to fire back."

Her jaw flexes, her eyes soften — and just like that, I've got her closer to breaking than Jace has gotten all night.

She breathes in slowly, like she's bracing for something, then says it.

"Marco."

The name's sharp enough to cut through the low diner hum.

I tilt my head, watching her. "And Marco is…?"

Her gaze flicks toward the window again before she looks back at me. "Cartel. And....My ex-fiancé."

Lucian's presence sharpens instantly — a predator scenting blood.

*Cartel? I've got a list of ways to handle that, and none of them involve talking.*

I keep my tone steady. "Why's he after you?"

Her fingers tighten around the coffee mug, eyes drifting to the window again. "Because I took something from him."

*Money? Drugs?* Lucian's voice is hungry. *We can flip it, make it ours.*

*We're here to help her, not exploit her.* Jace chimes in.

*Nothing wrong with making a quick buck or two.* Lucian replies.

*NO!* Jace says.

She shakes her head before I can even ask. "It's not about money. It was...a gift. A hair brooch clip. Gold. Diamonds. Been in my family for generations."

That makes me lean back. This isn't just theft — this is an insult.

*Yeah,* Lucian mutters darkly, *he's not coming for it. He's coming for her blood.*

I lean forward, elbows on the table, catching her eyes and holding them there. "Madz, you realize what that means, right? This isn't about getting back what you took. It's about punishing you for taking it."

She nods once, slowly.

Lucian's pacing in my head now. *We can end this before it starts. Track him. Trap him.*

*Not yet,* I tell him. *We move too early, we lose her trust. We need her to give us the whole story.*

I meet her gaze again, voice firm. "You're not facing Marco alone. That's not a request. You said he's after you because of the brooch. Tell me why you took it."

She keeps her eyes down, tracing the rim of her coffee like she's trying to hypnotize herself into a different conversation.

"Because it was mine before it was ever his to give. My grandmother's. She sold it to pay for my mother's medical bills. His family bought it. When he gave it to me, he acted like it was some grand romantic gesture." She scoffs. "It wasn't. It was him reminding me I'd always owe him."

Lucian growls low in my head. *So, she took it back. I like her more already.*

I nodded once. "And now he thinks taking you back evens the score."

Her lips press tight. She doesn't confirm it, but she doesn't have to. That's the thing about truths, if they're heavy enough, you can hear them drop even when no one says a word.

I lean back, stretch an arm along the back of the booth. Casual posture. Calculated. "How close is he?"

That gets me her eyes. They're not relaxed now — they're sharp, reading me, maybe deciding if I can handle the answer. "Closer than I thought. He's got people in this city. Watching."

Lucian's voice is eager now. *Then we start watching them.*

I shake my head slightly. "Name me one of his people."

She hesitates. Long enough that I know she's running through the list and weighing which name won't get me killed or get her burned. Finally — "Jorge. Tall. Shaved head. Scar over his right eye. Drives a black Suburban."

My brain files it away. Details like that don't get lost in me.

"If I see him, do I play nice?"

She almost laughs at that. "If you see him, you won't have time to play."

The corner of my mouth twitches. "We'll see about that."

Jace stirs, wanting to reassure her. I keep him in the backseat. She doesn't need comfort. She needs to know I'll do what needs doing.

"Madz," I say, leaning forward, lowering my voice so the diner hum swallows it, "if you want to end this, you're gonna have to give me more than crumbs. I need the whole map — who he trusts, where he moves his people, where he sleeps."

Her eyes soften, just for a breath. "That's not a map you can walk away from once you have it."

I smile, slow and deliberate. "Good thing I'm not the walking-away type."

We sit there, eyes locked, and for the first time tonight I feel her deciding, not if she should trust me, but how much. It's a start.

She finishes her coffee, sets the mug down. "I'll think about it."

I nod once. No push. You can't drag someone into trust —
you make the ground solid enough for them to step onto it
themselves.

We slide out of the booth and head for the door. The neon
hum follows us outside into the cool night air. We walked a
ways down the street to her hotel. She turns to face me
before we part ways, a faint smirk curling her lips.

"You're not what I expected," she says.

I step closer, just enough to let her see I'm not flinching.
"Good."

She leans in and kisses me — not soft, not quick, but
lingering, like she's planting a marker on a map I'm going to
keep following.

When she pulls back, there's something new in her eyes.
Not trust yet. But something close enough to be dangerous.

"Goodnight, Michael."

# Marco's Ire-The Wolf Outside

New York's cold hits different at this hour — it's quieter, meaner, like it's holding its breath before the next storm. I've been leaning against this brick wall long enough for the frost to cling to my jacket sleeves, boots planted where I can see her building without standing out.

The street's empty except for the occasional car sliding past, headlights flashing off the wet pavement. Then the door opens.

She steps out first. Hair a little messy, cheeks flushed. There's a glow in her eyes I've seen before — not in years, but I know it. It's the look she used to have after nights we didn't want to end.

And he's right behind her. Taller than me, dark hair, built like he's been in fights his whole life, and hasn't lost a single one. His jacket hangs open just enough to show the easy confidence in the way he moves — a man who's comfortable anywhere. That makes him dangerous.

They walk close. Not holding hands, but it's there — the

kind of closeness you don't fake. I notice her hair shifts when the wind catches it, and the glint of gold and silver peeks through. My jaw tightens. The brooch. She's still wearing it.

She laughs at something he says. Soft, short, like she doesn't want it to be heard. He glances at her with that protective look, the kind that says he'd stand between her and anything. I almost step forward right there.

Almost.

But patience has kept me alive when other men wound up with flowers on their graves. So I stay in the shadows, letting the night wrap around me. They head toward the pier — slow, unhurried. Like they've got nowhere else they'd rather be.

The wind bites through the open collar of my shirt, stinging the scar across my throat. A reminder. I don't rush. I don't swing first unless I'm sure I'll be the last man standing.

She's running from me — I can see it in the way she scans the street every few steps. But she's making the same mistake she made before. Thinking distance means safety.

I push off the wall, falling into step far enough behind that the sound of my boots gets swallowed by the city. I don't need to catch them tonight.

I just need to see where they go, and who he is to her.

And when the time's right, I'll take back what's mine.

The pier glows in that dull yellow haze that makes everything look older than it is. They walk slow, like they're trying to stretch the night out, shoulders brushing when the wind pushes them together. I keep my pace even, every step timed so I'm just a shadow in the spaces between streetlamps.

They don't linger long at the water. A few quiet words, a smile from her, a look from him that I don't like. Then they turn toward the diner a block over — the one with the flickering neon sign that can't decide if it's open or closed.

I take the long way around, crossing the street to slip behind a parked delivery van. The windows of the diner throw light onto the wet sidewalk, making it shine.

Inside, they sit in a booth by the window. She takes the seat facing out, coffee mug cupped in both hands like she needs the warmth. He leans back at first, then shifts forward, elbows on the table, voice low but steady.

I can't hear them, but I've learned to read more in movement than in words. She looks away when he pushes, not the kind of avoidance that comes from lying, but the kind that comes from not wanting to bleed in front of someone. He keeps pressing anyway.

Good. Let him dig. Let him think he's getting somewhere. Every question he asks now will make it easier when I finally decide to take her back.

Then I see it, her guard slips. Not much, just enough for her to say something that makes him freeze, then lean in closer. His hand shifts on the table, not quite touching her but damn near.

She's telling him about me.

Her fingers brush the brooch while she talks, like she doesn't even realize she's doing it. My jaw aches from holding still. The glass between us is the only thing keeping me from crossing the street.

The waitress comes, drops a check, says something that makes her smile again. He reaches for his wallet. They both stand, pulling on jackets. She tucks her hair back, the brooch catching the diner's neon for a heartbeat before the door swings shut behind them.

I don't follow right away. I watch them walk off into the cold, his arm brushing hers, her eyes scanning the street one last time. She doesn't see me.

Not yet.

I give them a thirty-second head start before stepping off the curb. The cold cuts through my jacket, biting harder now, but it keeps me sharp. Their pace is unhurried, like they've got all the time in the world.

He walks on the street side, casual but deliberate, the kind of man who's always places himself in front of the danger. That alone tells me too much about him. He's not just a distraction. He's protection. And protection can be broken.

They head down toward the busier stretch of the street, the neon from closed shops bleeding into puddles on the sidewalk. Her laughter carries back to me on the wind, lighter than it was earlier. Whatever he said in that diner, it chipped away at her defenses.

I stay in the flow of the city — a couple walking their dog gives me cover for half a block, then a pair of drunks arguing about the Knicks takes me the rest of the way. When the street thins out, I slip into a recessed doorway, letting them pass under the yellow glow of the last working streetlight on the block.

They slow near the corner. She turns to him, hands buried

in her coat pockets, face tilted up just enough that I catch the faintest curve of a smile. He leans down and says something I can't hear. Then she kisses him, not rushed, not hesitant. Certain.

It hits me harder than I expected.

When they part, she brushes his arm before heading toward her place. He waits until she disappears inside, then turns in the opposite direction. I watch both of them vanish into the night before stepping out of the shadows.

I know where she lives. I've seen his face.

And now, I've seen the crack in her armor.

Patience wins wars. This one has already begun.

# Slippery Shadows

*(Michael's pov)*

The click of her door echoes in my head longer than it should. One second she's right there, warm breath in the cold air, and the next she's gone, leaving nothing but the faint trace of her perfume and the feel of her mouth on mine.

I stand there a beat too long, eyes on the closed door, letting the quiet settle. Jace is the first to stir in the back of my head, all soft edges and second-guessing. *You could've eased up on her. She's already—*

*Already what?* I say as I turn to head home. The street's damp, that slick shine under the streetlamps making it look cleaner than it is.

Lucian chuckles low. *She's already in. Whether she knows it or not.*

I shove my hands into my jacket pockets and start walking, boots hitting the pavement in a steady rhythm. The city's got that in-between feel, not quite dead, but slow, like everyone's holding their breath for something they can't name. Perfect time to think.

Marco. Cartel. A brooch that's worth more than most people's houses. And a woman who's smart enough to know the danger but still stubborn enough to keep it close. That's not bad news for me. That's an opportunity.

A car passes, headlights dragging shadows across the buildings. My eyes track the reflections in the windows, habit more than paranoia.

Jace sighs in my head. *You're already moving pieces you don't have the board for.*

*That's how you win,* I tell him. *You start playing before they know they're in the game.*

The wind cuts around the corner, carrying the smell of old fry oil and something sweet from the bakery two blocks down. I take it in slowly, breathing through the cool bite of it. No rush now. I've got the breadcrumb, and it's bigger than she meant to give.

Lucian's voice sharpens. *We need eyes on him before he puts eyes on us.*

He's right, but that's tomorrow's problem. Tonight's about locking down what I've learned and figuring out just how far I can push her before she bolts.

The diner's neon hum is long behind me now, the streets thinning out as I cut toward my own corner of the city. Hands still in my pockets, chin down against the cold, but my mind's lit up like it's mid-fight.

Patience. She's not ready to hand me the map. But she will. They always do.

A ways down the block, something shifts in the air. Not sound, not sight, just that predator sense. The one you only get after years of walking streets where the wrong turn can get you buried.

I don't look back. Not yet.

Jace stirs. *You feel that?*

*Yeah,* I murmur, keeping my stride lazy. My eyes scan reflections in darkened storefronts, the warped chrome of a parked bike. There — half a block back, on the edge of the light.

Tall. Broad shoulders. Military haircut. The kind of posture that says he's not here by accident.

Lucian's voice sharpens. *Marco.*

Could be. Fits Madz's description well enough, and the way he's tracking my pace without closing the gap? Amateur moves for anyone else, but for him it's bait. He wants me to know he's there.

I keep walking. Turn right at the next block without breaking rhythm. I don't speed up, nor do I slow down. Let him think I'm just taking the long way home.

Street noise thins. My shadow lengthens under the next streetlight. In the corner of my eye, his angle shifts, following.

Jace is tight in the back of my head now. *We could just confront him. Get this over with.*

*Not my play tonight,* I tell him. *You confront too soon and you tip your hand.*

I cut down a narrow side street between two closed bodegas. The smell of damp cardboard and fryer oil lingers here, no cameras, no foot traffic. Good place for a fight. I keep moving anyway.

Lucian's grin is audible. *He's gonna think you're leading him somewhere.*

*Exactly.* I say. And then, halfway down, I slip between a stack of pallets and a dented delivery door, cutting sharp into the alley that runs parallel to the main street. The cold hits harder here.

Two turns later, I'm back in the city's regular heartbeat, merging into a knot of late-night pedestrians spilling out of a bar. Voices loud, laughter sharper than the air. Perfect cover.

I glance back once in the reflection of a dark SUV. Street's clean. He took the bait and lost the trail.

Jace exhales in relief. *You think he bought it?*

*He didn't buy it,* I say, turning my collar up against the wind. *He'll know I spotted him. But he won't know how much I saw.*

Lucian's low chuckle rides shotgun in my head. *Good. Let him wonder.*

I fade into the flow of the crowd, my mind already spinning the next move. Marco's here, he's watching, and now he knows I'm not the kind of prey that freezes in the open. Patience. Let him keep looking. The more he searches, the more I'll see.

The crowd thins as I cut through two more blocks, letting the cold air clear the last of Marco's scent from my head. The city's quieter here, the kind of stretch where the streetlights hum louder than the traffic.

The apartment's not far, and I keep it casual all the way, no sharp turns, no extra glances over my shoulder. If he's still out there, he's not close enough to matter.

We step inside and lock up. The deadbolt clicks, and with it, the night's tension starts to drain. Jace exhales in the back of my head, like he's been holding his breath the whole time.

*Are you sure we lost him?* He asks skeptically.

*Yeah,* I tell him, hanging the jacket on the hook by the door. *Even if we didn't, he's not dumb enough to make a move here.*

The apartment's dim, quiet. The kind of quiet that lets your pulse slow back to normal. I toe off my boots, head straight for the bed, and drop into it like the city's weight just slid off my shoulders.

Lucian mutters low, still keyed up. *We should've ended it tonight.*

*Not ready,* I say, stretching out. *Tomorrow's another day.*

Jace is calmer now, but I can feel his mind still running circles, replaying the tail, the angles, the what-ifs. I let him. Some people need to overthink to sleep, I just need four walls and enough heat to keep the chill from creeping in.

The room's warm enough, but the cold still clings to me when I stretch out on the bed, the sheets pull tight under my hands as I settle in.

Outside, the city keeps breathing. Somewhere out there, Marco's planning his next move.

Good. So am I.

I send a quick text to Jack and set my phone down. Sleep comes easy after that.

Jack's text pings at 8:11 a.m.

Jack: Your guy's out. Black Suburban. West 38th by the freight doors. Scar over right eye. Looks bored. Not alone.

Looks like my little favor I asked paid off.

I swing my legs off the mattress. Jace groans somewhere in the back of my head, the kind of tired that lives in the bones.

*Coffee first,* he mutters.

*Street first. Coffee on the move.*

*Fine. But don't make it that burnt motor oil you call espresso.*

Lucian's presence slides in like a shadow moving across a wall. *If it's Jorge, he'll sweep twice before committing. Expect a loop. Expect watchers.*

*I'm counting on it.*

I'm dressed in two minutes—dark denim, neutral jacket, cap low. We step out into the kind of winter morning that stings your nose hairs and makes the whole city smell like iron and wet concrete. Steam hisses from a sewer hole. A box truck coughs to life. Midtown's already grinding.

I snag a street coffee from a cart, Jace grumbles but drinks it. We cut east, then south, then west again, running my own lazy "S" to make sure no one's running one on us. By the time I hit 38th, the river's wind shoved the cloud cover into one flat sheet of pewter.

That's him from the description Madz gave.

Jorge leans on the Suburban's fender beneath a row of busted loading-bay lamps—tall, shaved head, scar over the right eye like a pale punctuation mark. He's got that ex-military stillness, the kind that reads as "harmless" right up until it doesn't. Two other men pretend to be interested in a shipping manifest. One keeps scratching his beard with the same two fingers, nervous tick or signal, can't tell yet.

*Street side cameras at the corner,* Lucian notes. *Don't get face-on. We'll use reflections.*

I slid into the shadow of a storefront window and watch

him through our ghost in the glass. Jorge checks his watch, checks the mouth of the alley, checks the rooftops. Not just counter surveillance, ritual. He's marking time for something.

Jace's voice softens. *He may appear cold, but he's human.*

*Human doesn't mean harmless,* I say, and move.

We tail loose, never behind him for more than half a block, always with bodies between us. He does what pros do: walks past his own Suburban to a bus stop, pretends to read the service changes, lets one bus go, boards the next. I don't chase a ride; I chase angles. Two blocks east, I grab a Citi Bike and ghost the bus from parallel avenues, catching him again through the windshield at each stoplight like he's a fish surfacing for air.

He hops off at 10th and 23rd, and melts into a pack of dog-walkers. He doesn't pet a single animal. That's how I know he's thinking too hard.

He cuts south along the High Line stairs, ducks under, pauses in the underpass shadow long enough to let anyone lazy overshoot. I don't. I spin the bike into a fading bike-lane stencil, set a lazy foot on the curb, pretend to tie a lace. He lights a cigarette he won't smoke, lets it burn down for a count of twenty, then flicks it into a puddle without looking back.

*He knows he's being watched by someone,* Lucian says. *Not sure who though.*

*Good, Let's make sure it isn't us.* I say.

He slides into a deli that's got more lottery ads than customers. I enter three doors down, buy gum I won't chew, and post where I can see the deli mirror. When he comes out, he's got a to-go bag and a new tail, a man in a green knit cap who stares too hard at nothing.

*Cap's not with us,* I murmur.

*He's not with us,* Lucian agrees. *But he's with someone.*

We dance like that for two hours.

Jorge runs a carousel nobody asked to ride: west to 11th, south to 14th, east to 7th Ave, then back west again. He doesn't text. He doesn't call. He just... exists. A ghost with places to be and all the time in the world to not be seen getting there.

At noon he finally gives me something.

Warehouse row, Meatpacking, bricks the color of dried blood, windows blanked from the inside. He raps three short, one long on a steel door like he's knocking on an old friend. The slot opens, an eye appears, then the door snicks and he disappears.

I don't move closer. I move wider.

Across the street: a vegan bakery with tiny tables and plants hanging like chandeliers. I buy the last croissant that tastes like nothing and take a window seat where the glare makes me but a smear. From here I see the street, the door, the corners, the rooftop edges. I draw the map in my head because paper gets you killed: camera over the awning (east-facing), two sightlines from the alley, one covered by a dumpster, one by a stack of skids. The fire escape ladder is chained. Fire hydrant's capped with a false lock, fast wrench work if you've got it. The Suburban hasn't moved. The man with the green knit cap reappears, swaps for a man in a denim jacket with an earpiece half-hidden by hair he can't afford.

Jace's voice is quiet when he speak. *If this is a staging point, we should walk away and plan. No cowboy moves.*

*Relax,* I say. *I'm just memorizing the exits.*

Lucian hums, approving. *If he comes out hot, let him go. We want his pattern, not his pulse.*

The door cracks at 12:26. A kid in a hoodie steps out, tosses a flattened Amazon box onto the skids. The kid's left sleeve rides up, ink peeks: a tiny angel with a knife. Not cartel. Street-level crew who like saints with sharp edges. Useful to know who's subcontracting.

Jorge emerges at 12:31 with nothing he didn't have going in. No package. No briefcase. No change in jacket weight. The tell is smaller, his shoulders drop one notch. He got what he came for, and it fit in his head.

He heads south again. I let two pedestrians and a delivery guy drift between us, then I follow. He rides the edge of the sidewalk like a man who hates windows. If he glances left, I glance right. If he jaywalks, I let a taxi horn write me into the street noise and cross on the red like a local ghost.

We spend the afternoon in motion.

Chelsea to the Village. The Village to SoHo. SoHo back west until the river smell gets big in the lungs. He takes coffee he doesn't drink, a sandwich he eats in four bites, a piss in a bar I won't walk into because the bouncer clocks faces like he's a human hard drive.

Twice he stops at street vendors and buys nothing. Once he stands in front of a pawn shop and looks at his own reflection for a full ten seconds like he's trying to remember the shape of himself. Every fifteen minutes he checks rooftops. Every twenty he checks his watch. Every thirty he scratches the scar like an itch that itches when he lies.

By 3:40 my fingers are thawed by friction and spite, and Jace runs out of reasons we should have stayed home. *You're right,* he concedes. *He's not aimless. He's waiting for a clock we can't see.*

At 4:05 we get a near-burn.

Crosswalk at Varick. Light changes. A bus blocks the far side for three beats and when it rolls, Jorge is angled back toward us, chin high, eyes sweeping the crowd. He doesn't stop. He just lets the stream part around him, and for a clean second, we're in his kill box.

Jace's breath hitches. *Don't look down. Don't break stride.*

I don't. I raise my phone and catch my reflection in the black glass like I'm checking a text that doesn't exist. Lucian counts in my head. *Three... two... one...*

The moment passes. He slides by, eyes already past us, already on the next window and the one after that. Somebody else gets nervous. Not me.

By 5:10, the city lights its evening face. Storefronts bloom.

Tail-lights string out like a necklace no one can afford. The air picks up a knifes edge—the kind that finds the gap between your scarf and your collar and takes root.

That's when the gravity changes.

I feel her before I see her. It's not magic. It's repetition. People have signatures and hers is a frequency that lives somewhere behind my sternum, a low note that finds the places I keep for fire and sharp things.

She's up ahead, coming toward us along the river path—hair pinned back by a glint that used to belong to another man, coat belted, chin up against the cold. She's scanning like always, but softer—more "where are you" than "who's coming." Her eyes find me. She knows immediately which of us she's getting.

"Madz." I say when we meet at the bend in the rail. I don't touch her. Not yet.

Her mouth curves, wry. "You stalking me or working?"

"Both."

She huffs a small laugh and then her gaze flicks past me, over my shoulder, out into the slow-moving crowd where the day commuters are turning into night versions of themselves.

"Walk with me," she says.

We fall in step, hands brushing once, not by accident. I angle us so I can use the glass of a bus shelter and the river as twin mirrors. Two joggers pass. A cyclist curses at the wind. From the corner of the shelter's reflection, I catch a shape I've come to know, denim jacket, hair hiding an earpiece. Not Jorge. One of his satellites.

*We've got a friend orbiting,* Lucian notes.

*Let him.* I say. *We're not here to be ghosts. We're here to teach them how bad it feels to think they see us.*

Jace lifts his head inside. *We should take her off the line. Safer to talk under a ceiling.*

*Agreed.* I nod toward the street.

"Diner or home?"

Madison doesn't miss the subtext. She tips her head, choosing, thinking, measuring what each option means. Then she glances at me through the lashes like she always does when she's about to pick the path with the higher cliff.

"Home," she says.

"Good," I tell her, and we turn east, away from the water, away from the joggers and the watchers and the Suburban that will eventually appear where Suburban's always do.

We don't hurry. We don't dawdle. We move like people who belong to the city and to ourselves. Jorge's satellite keeps a respectful, ignorant distance, comforted by our lack of urgency. That's the thing about menace, most men only recognize it when it's yelling.

At 5:29 we cut left, then right, then through a lobby that smells like lemon cleaner and other people's heat. The elevator doors slide open with a tired sigh. I press the button for our floor.

As the doors begin to close, I catch denim jacket in the mirror-finish, pausing at the corner like he's deciding whether to make a religion out of bad choices.

He doesn't.

The doors meet. The cable hums. The numbers climb.

Jace exhales and some tension leaves finally, some other kind arriving. *She came with us. That means trust, or exhaustion, or both.*

Lucian's voice is quiet steel. *It means we plan, then we hunt.*

I look down at Madison. She looks back up at me, tired, fierce, unflinching. The kind of woman wars get started over and ended for.

"Inside," I say when the doors part. "We'll eat, we'll talk, we'll sleep. Tomorrow, we make someone else tired."

She smiles, small and real. "Bossy."

"Effective."

# Wine And Dine

The door shuts behind us with a heavy click, sealing the city out. My place isn't fancy, but it's mine — dim lighting, leather couch with just enough wear to be comfortable, the low hum of the fridge from the kitchen.

I drop my jacket on the arm of the couch, toss my keys into the ceramic dish by the door. She takes it in with that subtle glance women give when they're cataloging details, the photos on the shelf, the scuff marks on the floor, the fact that everything's in its place without being spotless.

*"Never really got a chance to look around last time I was here."* She says.

I can feel Lucian's smirk.

*Shut up!*

*I didn't say a word.* He says smugly

"Are you hungry?" I ask, already heading for the kitchen.

Her smile tilts. "Starving. But not sure for what yet."

The fridge opens, and I pull out leftover steak and roasted

potatoes from the night before. Skillet hits the stove, butter melting into a slow hiss. She leans against the counter, close enough that I catch the faint trace of her perfume over the smell of searing meat.

"You cook?" she asks, teasing.

I glance at her over my shoulder. "I do a lot of things. Cooking's just one of them."

She laughs low, takes the wine bottle I set out and pours two short glasses. We eat standing up at the counter, steaks cut into bite-sized pieces, potatoes crisp and salty. The wine's smooth, loosening the edges without dulling the tension.

"You're a terrible influence," she says after her second glass.

"Guilty," I reply, leaning in just enough for my voice to drop. "But you like it."

Her eyes hold mine for a second too long before she turns toward the couch. I follow the easy way she moves, making it feel like she's already been here before. Oh, right.

Lucian smirks again. I visibly roll my eyes.

We sit close enough that her knee brushes mine when she shifts. The TV stays off. The wine keeps flowing. Our conversation slips from light jabs into quieter territory, hints of what we've been through without spelling it all out.

At some point, she tucks her legs under her, facing me fully. "You're not what I expected," she says softly.

I lean in just enough that she feels the warmth of my breath when I answer. "Good."

The space between us narrows, slow and deliberate. My hand brushes her knee, then her thigh. She doesn't move away, in fact she leans closer, her smile turning into something hungrier.

The wine's working its way through her system, but she's not sloppy, she's warm. The edges of her guardedness starting to curl back. Her knees are still tucked under her, angled toward me, and that smirk she had when we walked in hasn't left.

"You're staring," she says.

"Observing," I correct, letting my gaze trace the line of her throat down to the faint shadow where her blouse dips. "Big difference."

Her lips twitch like she wants to challenge it, but the glass in her hand buys her a moment. She takes a slow sip.

I shift just enough to rest my arm along the back of the

couch, close enough that if she leans back, my fingers will be brushing her shoulder. She doesn't lean away.

"You always bring women here after a stakeout?" she asks.

"No," I say, voice low, letting the word hang there. "You're the exception."

She glances down at her glass again, but her smile gives her away. The air between us changes, heavier, more deliberate.

I take her glass, set it on the coffee table. She protests and picks it back up. Her eyes stay on me, watching what I'll do next.

I let my knuckles skim up her thigh, slow enough that she has to choose whether to stop me. She doesn't.

Jace is there in the back of my head, quiet but restless. *Don't rush her.*

*I'm not rushing.* I say. I'm reading her, the subtle shift of her breathing, the way her eyes flicker between my mouth and my eyes.

"You're staring," she says, a faint smirk tugging her lips.

"I'm running the math," I answer, letting my grin creep in. "Angles, timing, proximity. Science, really."

She laughs, low. "And what's the equation say?"

"That if you take another sip, you're gonna lean just far enough for me to catch you."

Her eyebrow arches. "Catch me doing what?"

"That," I point, as she tilts her glass and her shoulder dips closer to me without her noticing. "Exactly that."

She sets her wine down, shaking her head like she's not going to give me the satisfaction. But her knee brushes mine, and I file away the way she doesn't move it.

"You're trouble," she says.

"I'm a solution," I correct, eyes locking on hers. "The trouble's you."

That earns me a slow smile, one I know means keep going.

"I'm also good at reading people," I say. "And right now, you're thinking about it."

Her voice drops half a tone. "Thinking about what?"

"Whether you're gonna kiss me first," I murmur, leaning just enough that my breath brushes her cheek, "or make me work for it."

She laughs again, softer this time, and it rolls right into the space between us. She turns her head just as I turn mine. Our mouths crash into one another. She tastes like morning sunshine after winter's first touch in New York. I can taste the wine, sweet but tart.

She pulls back and gazes into my eyes. Her eyes look like they're on fire. Sweetheart, I'm willing to burn in them. She gives me a look that says 'I dare you to stop'.

I get up from the couch, bringing her with me. Our mouths crash together again.

"To the bedroom," I say "now"

She stops and sits back down, pulling on my shirt, bringing me back down with her.

"No, I want you right here. On the couch. So, whenever the others see it, they'll all have a reminder." She says with a wink.

I don't argue, I start ripping off clothes. My shirt first, then her pants. I help her out of her blouse and stare at her full luscious bra clad breast.

"If you're only going to stare I guess I…" she starts to say but I lean and capture her neck with my mouth. She moans. I slightly tilt my head up, "I don't think you want to finish that sentence Madz."

Her bra drops to the floor a second later, then her underwear. She's lying on the couch, with me pressed against her.

I waste no time exploring her body. I start with her throat. Kissing and nipping at her, making her moan. I kiss my way down to her breast, stopping at her peaks and sucking one hardened bud into my mouth.

Breathing heavy she exclaims. "Yes, more, harder."

I oblige, I'm nothing if not a gentleman.

I take the other bud into my mouth and give it a little bite. She yelps and digs her hands into the cushions. Sounds of ecstasy leave her mouth as I kneed and massage her breast. Toying with her nipples.

I keep her distracted, while one of my hands slips lower. I find that small little bundle of nerves and gently press on it. She gasps. Looking into my eyes, she smiles. That's all the invitation I need. I slip one finger in while I let my thumb work her clit. I can feel her muscles clenching and releasing.

She's breathing heavier now as I put one more finger in, my thumb still circling her clit. She gasps again. I keep working her, drawing out every sound imaginable. I lean in and kiss her, capturing those moans with my mouth. Her breath becomes mine.

Her back arches off the couch as she starts gyrating her hips, fucking herself on my fingers. I notice the moment she's about to come. Her inner walls gripping my fingers tight. Her breathing increases, faster and deeper.

"Yes, yes, yes" she starts chanting. And then it happens, she squirts, coating my hand with her juices.

I remove my hand slowly after letting her ride out her orgasm. Bringing my fingers to my mouth I lick and suck every digit clean. She doesn't take her eyes off me.

I'm about to remove my pants when she pushes me off her and drops to her knees. I go to stop her but she waves me off reaching for my belt. Then she does something I never thought possible.

I say 'I' because Lucian would have done this,

She gets my belt off and wraps it around her throat. I immediately go to stop her but she just smacks my hand away.

She undoes my jeans and drops them. Then pushes me back down on the couch.

"I trust you, Michael. I'll give you one squeeze to signal to tighten and two if I want you to loosen."

She says with a grin.

I look down at my belt wrapped around her throat and see the other end in my palm. I wrap it around my hand once. I give her a nod, and that's all she needs.

She licks the tip, tasting the small bit a pre-cum leaking out. Then she runs her tongue from base to tip, while cupping my balls and rolling them around in her palms.

She starts stroking me, then sucks the head into her mouth. I feel a squeeze. I pull on the belt just a little. She moans around my cock and I about cum right there. She takes me deeper, still stroking me.

She releases my balls and I see her hand start to play with her clit. I decide right then and there, I love watching this woman get herself off.

She increases her speed with both her mouth and her hand that's still pumping me. I feel another squeeze. I pull harder this time, then immediately I feel two squeezes back to back, and I let up a little. She moans in agreement. I throw my head back looking up at the ceiling and let out a moan myself. Damn this woman knows how to work me.

She is taking me as deep as she can now. I know because I

can feel me hitting the back of her throat. I look down and see her lips barely touch her hand on me. Tears are streaming down her face. I feel another squeeze. When I don't pull, she looks up, still sucking me. I can tell she wants this, but I've never done something like this before. Then I notice the look she's giving me, not me ....Lucian.

*She can handle it, give her what she wants. I promise she will be okay,* He says

I listen and pray to whatever god there is that he is right. I pull tighter, her fingers that are playing with her pussy start moving fast, Her head bobbing up and down more aggressively. Her hand on my dick pumping quicker. I'm about to explode in the back of her throat if she doesn't.....I hear her and feel her moan around my dick again and that does it for me.

"Madz, unless you want to swallow I suggest..." I say, but she gives me a look that says 'I swallow and love it'. I don't argue, I throw my head back and release down her throat. She swallows Every. Last. Drop. She even licked up the little bit the dribbled out the sides of her mouth, like my dick was a popsicle.

She slowly gets to her feet and straddles my lap. She takes her fingers that were just inside her and sucks on them. She doesn't waste time with small talk. Her lips are on mine in a heartbeat. I can taste her, and myself. I've never been so turned on after just coming.

I don't wait, I lift her up and position her over my cock and slam into her. Her nails dig into my back. I give her a minute to adjust.

I'm not a complete asshole. *Yes you are,* Jace says.

*Shut up!*

She starts to rock back and forth after releasing her death grip on my back. We stay there for a while, getting lost in the feel of one another.

I can tell she's getting worn out physically so I pick her up and flip her, so her ass is on the couch. I lay her down and continue to thrust into her. Her hips move with the motion. Eyes locked on me as she leans up and I reciprocate leaning in to kiss her. She still tastes like morning sunshine after winter's first touch in New York.

I'm completely lost in her. I can feel her nails start to dig into my back again. Her moans become louder, breathier. Each thrust working her up more and more. She's close again, and so am I.

I feel her pussy grip me tighter. She's clinging to me like I'm her last lifeline. Panting harder, louder, till she's screaming my name.

"Michael, please don't stop! Please don't....please....please." she says as she comes down from her orgasm. I spill inside her at that exact moment.

We lay there a little while longer, before I decided we needed to get cleaned up.

We make our way to the shower, "Ladies first," I say. She grabs my hand and pulls me in. Smiling, I let her. We go another round in the shower, making the water turn cold by the time we are done.

I checked the time...1:09am. Damn!

"Hey," I say "you're sleeping here tonight."

She doesn't argue. "Okay I can sleep on the couch."

"Why? You can just sleep in bed with me."

"Oh, you don't mind?" she asks.

"After what we just did, you could kick me to the couch and I wouldn't complain."

She smiles and leans against me, "No need for that, let's go to sleep."

I lead the way to the bedroom and pull the covers back. She slides in, and I follow suit. It's not long before her breathing even out, letting me know sleep has fully claimed her. And for the first time in what seems like an eternity, I let myself relax and just fall to sleep.

# Aftermath

*(Michael's Pov)*

I jerk awake. Something's wrong. The room is too still, too heavy, like the air itself is holding its breath. Madison's soft breathing is beside me, curled against the sheets. For half a second, I let myself look at her. Then I hear it again. A shift of weight. Right outside the door. My hand finds the knife on the nightstand. My fingers are steady, but my chest is burning. I rise slowly, every muscle tight, eyes fixed on the door. Then it explodes inward. They flood the room—masked, armed, eyes locked on Madison. Cartel. I don't think, I move. The blade is in my hand and I slash the first throat before his weapon even rises. Hot blood sprays across the wall. The second lunges at me and I drive the steel between his ribs and rip it free. I'm faster than I should be, stronger than I should be, and for a moment I think I can hold them. But there are too many. A boot catches me in the ribs, knocking the knife loose. I swing wild, fists cracking bone, but more pile on. A gunstock smashes across my shoulder, another across my jaw. I stumble, but I won't fall.

"Run!" I snarl, but Madison doesn't move fast enough. Hands grab her and drag her screaming towards the door. Rage tears through me, sharp and endless. I fight harder, clawing, biting, anything to keep standing, to keep them from taking her. But they slam me down, a boot grinding into my chest. Darkness consumes me when the final blow from the butt of a rifle collides with my head.

*(HIM's pov)*

The walls don't hold me. They mock me. Steel, chains, fire, none of it is real, yet all of it burns into my bones. And worse, worse than the prison itself, is the hand that keeps me here.

The other. Stronger. Always stronger. I don't even know who he is. How the hell he came to be.

He pushes me down like I'm nothing, like I'm some shadow caged in the back of his skull. And I hate him for it. I hate him with every shred of violence boiling in my veins. I could split the earth open with my fury and still it wouldn't be enough.

And then I feel it.

Not him. Not me. Them.

Footsteps. Breaths against the door. Death has come, dragging its stink into our den, and it isn't for him, it's for her.

*Madison.*

The rage detonates inside me. I slam into the bars until they bend. I claw at the walls until blood coats my hands, though there's no blood here to give. I scream, I roar, I tear, but the chains tighten until I can taste iron in my mouth.

*Wake up!* I thunder into his skull, my voice a storm that shakes the cage. *WAKE! UP!*

But he stirs like a drunk. A fool. Too slow. Too weak.

I rage harder. My body isn't mine, my hands can't cut, but I tear anyway. I hurl myself against the walls until my bones crack. Until the cage shudders. Until the whole prison feels like it's about to collapse.

The bars rattle with every slam of my fists, but they do not break. They only echo my rage back at me, taunting, laughing, feeding the fire that devours me. My hands are bone and iron; I smash until sparks of agony streak through my arms, but there is no blood, no ruin. Only the walls. ALWAYS THE WALLS.

And through the cracks of this cursed prison, I see him.

Michael. Weak, staggering, knife in his hand, but it trembles. Too slow.

I snarl until my voice is nothing but raw fire. The roar shakes the marrow of this cage, but still he doesn't hear me. He moves, strikes, the first hits landing as phantom chains cinch tighter, biting into my throat.

The cartel swarms him, boots and fists and steel, and all I can do is watch. *MARCO!* Rage tears me apart, slamming me against the walls until cracks spider through the stone. My fists crater the surface, my claws rake deep grooves, and I swear the air itself is splitting with me.

*You useless shell!* I thunder, the words ripping through the void. *YOU LET THEM TOUCH HER!*

Madison's scream rips through the dark. It shatters me. I tear at the bars until my hands are nothing but shards of fire and bone. I slam until the world blurs white. I thrash until I can't tell if the cage is breaking or if I am.

And still, the other presence holds me down. Stronger. Unyielding. Mocking. My power burns, my fury detonates, and yet, I remain caged. Forced to choke on the sight of Michaels failure, when every part of me knows I could end them in seconds if only I were free.

The taste of iron floods my mouth. My roar shakes the blackend walls until they bleed dust. But the cage remains.

Michael falls. Madison is taken.

And I am left with nothing but rage, enough to split the earth.

The calm comes last. Cooling into a white-hot fire simmering beneath my skin.

*They took her. From him. From ME.* My voice cracks.

They will pay.

EVERY! LAST! ONE!

# Author's Thank You

Every story may begin in the imagination of one person, but
it takes the strength of others to help bring it to life.

To my editor and friend, Brittany–thank you for standing
by me, sharpening my words, and reminding me of the voice
I didn't always think I had. This book would not exist in its
truest form without your dedication, patience, and honesty.
You pushed me to make this better, and for that, I am
endlessly grateful.

And to my readers–thank you for stepping into the dark
with me. Your time, your belief, and your willingness to
trust me with your imagination means more than I can ever
say. This journey is only beginning, and I'm honored to
have you walking it with me.